LIVE OAK KEY

Also by Kevin Matthew Hayes

Inspirational/Western
Ethan Tucker's Job

All Hallows' Eve Tales
The Beast of Talbotton
Reckonings
Facing Demons

Poetry
Summer 2020
July 4, 2020
Day Dreaming
The Forts of Pensacola Bay
Nightfall at Pensacola Beach
Blackwater River State Park
Are You Prepared for All Hallows' Eve?
The Legend of Ole Stingy Jack

Live Oak Key

KEVIN MATTHEW HAYES

ISBN: 978-1-965315-16-3 (paperback)
ISBN: 978-1-965315-17-0 (hardcover)
ISBN: 978-1-965315-18-7 (e-book)

This is a work of fiction. Names, characters, businesses, places, events, locales, and incidents are either the products of the author's imagination or used fictitiously. Any resemblance to actual persons, living or dead, or actual events is purely coincidental.

Proofread by:
Proofed.com

Book cover design and layout by:
Ellie Bockert Augsburger / CreativeDigitalStudios.com

Cover design features stock images by:
PlatypusMi86 / stock.adobe.com
paul / stock.adobe.com
waqar / stock.adobe.com

Author portrait by:
Matt Keene / St. Augustine Tintype

Published by Live Oak Key Publishing LLC

www.liveoakkeypublishingllc.com

Live Oak Key Publishing LLC was established in July 2024 by author Kevin Matthew Hayes. His passion is to publish stories based on the history, legends, and culture of the American South and American West.

Visit our website to shop other titles and merchandise, and follow our socials.

~ 1 ~

"BEWARE THE IDES OF MARCH."

A monument of a gray horse rearing stood in front of the immaculate Roman-like entrance. It was the calling card of the International Equestrian Park, graced by the fortunes of the wealthy from around the world. Luxury vehicles lined the road leading to the imposing entrance as the uniformed guard in the security booth verified each of the drivers before allowing them entry into the facility. The sun was beginning to set, and visitors were eager to see the first of the show jumpers competing for the title.

The diesel engine of my truck hummed away as I patiently waited my turn in line. I looked in my rearview mirror, past the window guard on the back of my cab. The driver behind me looked to be about in his thirties, like me. He was driving a red Ferrari and sitting back in his seat with a cool and collected expression. His left arm was propped out the window. He was wearing a white dress shirt with a sport jacket, and his eyes were hidden by his dark sunglasses. He leaned toward the steering wheel, examined the tailgate of my Ford, then rolled up his window before assuming the same position as before. He seemed displeased with the sight of the truck in front of him.

I looked ahead, and the boom gate lifted, allowing the car in front of me to enter. I pulled up to the window. The barrier lowered in front of my vehicle before disappearing out of view. The uniformed guard had his back to me.

"Howdy," I said.

The guard turned around. He was an older man with gray hair. His steam-pressed clothes looked like a full dress uniform for a police officer. I tipped my brown Stetson as a sign of respect. He took a small step back and looked at my truck, from the brush guard to the louvered tailgate. He had a stern look on his face.

"Horses are picked up on the other side of the facility," he said. He pointed in that general direction. "You should have saw the signs for the service road on your way in."

"No, sir," I replied. "I'm not here to pick up horses. I'm supposed to meet my client here." I pulled out my phone. The guard leaned over and looked at the screen. "I'm supposed to meet Mrs. Philippe."

"Yes, sir!" he said. "Right away." His stern look disappeared, and his attitude changed immediately.

"She must be a bigwig in these parts," I said. I was fishing for some gossip, but he didn't answer. He was more worried about disrupting Mrs. Philippe.

The guard turned, picked up his phone and asked for her room, and waited. Then he turned back to me. "Mrs. Philippe is one of our guests here at the park," he said. "She is the owner of Tempest and—" He stopped mid-sentence when he heard a voice from the other end of the line. I waited as they talked.

"What's your name?" he asked me.

"Colt Callacy, P.I." I replied. I reached into my wallet and presented my private investigator license to the guard. The guard took it with his free hand, examined it, and handed it back to me.

"It's Mr. Colton Callacy," he said into the phone.

"You can just call me Colt..."

"Yes, ma'am," the guard said. "Right away."

The guard hung up the phone and pressed a button, opening the barrier gate to let me through. "Just head down this drive until you reach the main building, Mr. Callacy. When you enter, the clerks at the front desk will escort you to Mrs. Philippe's suite."

"How will I know if I'm at the main building?"

"Believe me," replied the guard. "You can't miss it."

I put my truck in gear and pulled forward. The diesel exhaust whistled behind me as I accelerated. Massive Southern live oaks lined the way, their limbs stretching over the newly laid drive. Spanish moss peacefully swung back and forth high up in the branches. Situated along both sides of the drive were different stables and arenas. Riders were hard at work preparing their mounts for the first round of jumping scheduled for tonight.

After about a mile and a half, the road opened to a giant parking lot. Beyond that, tucked away among more oaks, was the main building of the International Equestrian Park. The guard was right: It was impossible to miss. It was a luxury hotel for the horse owners to stay in during the competitions. The main hotel was several stories tall, with large columns lining the entranceway. Topping it was a roof with high peaks. Together, the features gave the structure a classical and sophisticated look. The faint illumination of floodlights shining against the building could be seen as evening loomed over the facility—a sign the owners were proud of their investment and wanted all to see it, day or night.

I decided to park my truck at the back of the parking lot. It had a long wheelbase and took up two parking spots. As I stepped out of the truck, I looked around to get my bearings. My dark truck stood out like a sore thumb among the sea of luxury cars.

After a small hike through the parking lot, I walked through the building's automatic glass doors. I removed my Stetson and looked up at the ceiling. A large crystal chandelier hung above the lobby, lighting the entire area. Then I scanned the room. Finely crafted furniture lined the lobby. Coffee tables sat in front of some of the seats, each displaying small statues of allegorical figures. I read the plaques of some as I walked by them: Parcae, Fortuna, Lustitia.

I was out of place for sure. My jeans and button-down shirt stood out among the designer apparel of the guests. My boots echoed throughout the room as I approached the desk. I kept my hat in my hand and dodged around the uniformed hotel workers who were hard at work escorting guests and moving luggage. An older woman looked up from behind the desk.

"Howdy," I said.

"Welcome to the International Equestrian Park of Ocala," she replied. "How can I help you?"

"My name is Colt Callacy. I'm here to see Mrs. Philippe."

"Yes," she said. "Mrs. Philippe is expecting you. She told us to send you right up." She turned to another one of the workers. "Please show Mr. Callacy to Mrs. Philippe's suite."

The attendant nodded his head in agreement. "Follow me," he said.

We took an elevator to the top floor. The doors opened to a long hall featuring a marble floor and chandeliers lighting the way. Pictures of famous equines lined the walls, a wood console table situated under each one. Mrs. Philippe was located in room two. The door seemed to tower over us both.

The attendant knocked lightly. After a few seconds, the door opened just enough to stretch the chain on the other side.

"Mrs. Philippe," said the attendant, "Mr. Callacy is here."

"Thank you," she replied in a French accent. Mrs. Philippe unchained the door and opened it. She looked right at me. "Please come in."

Mrs. Philippe was older and looked the part of a French aristocrat. She was wearing a sequined black gown, with white diamond earrings and a necklace to match. I could tell she was worried, but she didn't panic. She seemed to be trying to conduct herself in a conservative fashion.

"Thank you for coming on such short notice, Mr. Callacy."

"Please, Mrs. Philippe, call me Colt."

"If you wish," she replied. "Let me take your hat."

I thanked her, and she hung my Stetson on a coatrack at the entrance.

"Please have a seat," she said.

I looked around the suite. It looked just like the rest of the hotel. The living area had a tall ceiling with a chandelier. At the back of the suite were French doors leading to a balcony that oversaw the main arena below. The room was carefully furnished to show off the wealth of the hotel owners.

We both sat down and began discussing the case.

"Mrs. Philippe," I said. "You told me some of the details over the phone, but I am going to say it one more time: In a situation like this, we should get the police involved. It's not usual for a horse like this to be stolen. I would think that most thieves would be afraid of the publicity associated with it."

"I understand," she replied. "But my mare, Tempest, is scheduled to jump this Sunday. I'm afraid that if I get the police involved, we won't make it in time. They may want to hold the poor thing for legal matters. She is my late husband's show jumper. If he were here, he would do anything to let that horse compete. I want her to race to honor his legacy."

I paused for a minute.

"You seem determined for this horse to compete," I said. I pulled out my phone and began researching the mare. "Her name is Tempest?" I asked to verify. Since she was an international competitor, I knew I could easily find a detailed description of her.

"That's correct," Mrs. Philippe responded.

"Is this her?" I showed her a picture.

"That's my husband's Tempest," she answered.

Tempest was a black mare from the Chantilly, France, region. She had several awards to her name. She had never gone all the way to the top, though. I continued to scan the stats.

"Does she have a chip or marking?" I asked.

"No," Mrs. Philippe replied. "My husband couldn't bring himself to do it. He thought it was inhumane. She does have a scar on her right leg from an incident years back."

"She's twenty and still competing?" I asked. "Don't these horses usually retire before that age? The only reason I ask is because of that horrible episode with Hickstead."

"Mr. Colt," she said, "we're talking about my husband's horse." She began to tear up. "I want her to race one more time. For my husband."

"I'm sorry. When did your husband pass away?"

"Several months ago."

"I'm very sorry for your loss."

I paused for a moment so that Mrs. Philippe could gather herself. I felt bad and didn't know what to say. I decided to look at more of the stats on my phone and waited until she was ready to continue.

"Mrs. Philippe, I see Tempest has been here before. Has anything changed from the last time she was shipped to the US? Did you use a different transport company?"

"I don't know," she said. "I let Chambon handle the logistics."

Mr. Chambon entered the room on cue as if he had been waiting for his introduction. He was a clean-cut gentleman dressed in business attire.

"Good evening," he said in a Southern accent. He reached out to shake my hand.

"This is Colt," Mrs. Philippe said. "Colt, this is Chambon. He's been helping me handle some of my affairs since my husband's passing."

I stood up and shook the man's hand. "Your accent," I said. "You come from Louisiana."

"New Orleans," he replied.

"It sounds like the business sector."

"That's correct."

"I had a client with a similar accent one time before," I said. "I've always admired the accents of Louisiana."

We sat down, and I continued to gather information.

"Mr. Chambon," I began, "has anything changed from the last time Tempest was brought here? Was a different transport company used?"

"I used a new company," he said. "But they offered a lower price." He stood up, walked over to a desk, and looked over some paperwork. Then he handed me a file before sitting back down.

"Are you sure they are legit?" I said as I opened the file.

"Mr. Colt," Mrs. Philippe said, "I know Chambon." She placed her hand on his knee and looked at him. "I know he would never allow anyone to mistreat my husband's Tempest." I could see tears building up in her eyes again. "My late husband would be crushed."

I began leafing through the file and looked up the company with my phone. I didn't see anything suspicious.

"It's a legit company," I said. "It's a registered corporation. When was Tempest last seen?"

"She was last seen at customs," Chambon replied.

"You saw Tempest yourself?" I asked.

"Not exactly," he answered. There was a pause. "I was contacted by customs after she entered the country. She was flown in. They said they were transferring her to the quarantine facility."

"When was this?" I questioned.

"About two in the afternoon on Tuesday," he replied. "I then received another call saying that Tempest was going to leave the facility today at four. She was supposed to be delivered here to the park today around five in the afternoon."

"Did either one of you check Tempest at the facility?" I inquired.

"I just flew in this morning," chimed in Mrs. Philippe. "I was hoping to see her this afternoon."

I looked at Chambon. He just shook his head no before I looked down at my watch.

"It's eight o'clock now," I stated. "Why did you wait so long to call me?"

"At first, we weren't too worried," Chambon replied. "It's Friday afternoon, and we figured traffic was just bad. We started to worry after about an hour. We tried calling the facility, but we never received an answer. We were not sure how to handle the situation. Mrs. Philippe didn't want the police involved, as she stated." They looked at each other briefly. "We just want to get Tempest back so she can compete Sunday."

"Every minute counts in a situation like this," I said. "The more people involved, the better your chances of getting Tempest back."

"Mr. Colt," began Mrs. Philippe, "please, we don't want the police involved. My husband would be devastated if Tempest missed her last year competing. Please do it for my late husband. I want Tempest to compete one more year before she retires."

They both paused for a minute.

"Can you help us, Colt?" asked Chambon. "I know you must have a tight schedule. Some of the staff in the stables spoke highly of you. They said you had tracked down stolen horses before."

I sat back in my chair for a minute. I really didn't have a tight schedule. The fact of the matter was, I didn't have any clients at the moment. Two of my previous clients had yet to pay me, and money was tight. Still, this was a good time to barter.

"That's true," I said. "I've been hired by ranchers in the past to track down stolen horses. It doesn't happen very often. This is different, though. I've never tracked down such a prominent purebred." I paused and rubbed my chin with my fingers like I was thinking. I could feel my five-o'clock shadow. "It makes me wonder what type of people would steal a horse like this. It's not like you can sell it easily." I paused again, like I was debating in my head whether I wanted to take the case. "I do have a few clients right now. They keep me very busy."

"We'd be willing to pay you extra," blurted Mrs. Philippe. "Please do it for my late husband."

We discussed terms for a little while longer. Then I clasped my hands together and placed them against my chin before looking down at the floor like I was thinking. "I will have to put some of my current clients on hold, but considering the circumstances, I'm sure they'll understand."

"We have a deal?" asked Mrs. Philippe.

"I will get started immediately."

"Wonderful," she replied. We stood up and shook hands to approve the deal. "Please be careful. They might be dangerous."

"Beware the Ides of March," I replied. It was all that came to mind.

$$\sim 2 \sim$$

"IT'S A LONG SHOT, BUT IT'S A STARTING POINT."

The monotone sound of my truck's engine humming through the darkness was soothing to my ears. It helped me think about the case. I was debating where to start. As I approached the end of my trip, the condensation from the air conditioning began building on the windshield, obscuring my view ahead. Despite it, I could just make out the faint traces of the old "tin man"-style water tower with the red light on top. It had come to serve as a symbol for the rural community of Williston.

I rounded a curve lined with old streetlights illuminated by metal halide bulbs. The lights radiated a yellowish color that I remembered from my childhood, not like those white LED lights found in most cities today. Then I crossed the railroad tracks at the entrance of town. I looked over at the old train depot as I passed it. A light was on in one of the windows. The days of passenger service were long gone, and the building mainly served as an office for the workers now.

The railroad workers must be putting in a late night themselves, I thought to myself.

The railroad was an old short line, and the train managed to pass through town once a week. The locomotive's paint was faded and the engine was in desperate need of an overhaul. In fact, most of town could hear the old engine when it passed through with its few freight cars.

Williston was like any other small country town, but I was partial to it because it had served as my home for the past few years. It had a couple of traffic lights and the necessities. The auto stores were open late to serve farmers and ranchers. There was a hardware store, a feed store, and a barber shop that also served as meeting grounds to catch up on local gossip and get advice. There were some bars nearby where the cowboys were known to get rowdy. And the grocery store was always busy on Sundays after church. The town had been known to host parades on main street or events in the park to drum up business for the stores, celebrate the local high school team, or bring the community together during the holidays.

Old storefronts lined the main street. Behind them were neighborhoods that consisted of a mixture of new and old homes. The old brick structures at the center of town were a reminder of the old department stores and businesses that had flourished a century ago. Now, the storefronts seemed to be a mixture of established local businesses and revolving antique stores and restaurants; chain stores built their own structures further down the road.

I turned a corner once I'd almost reached the center of town and entered a large gravel parking lot situated behind the connected storefronts. I circled my truck around, then backed it behind one of the store's back doors. It was my office, which also served as my home. As I exited the truck, the humidity hit me like a thick wall. Everything was damp from the afternoon's thunderstorms. I felt my jeans and shirt stick to my skin. The crickets and cicadas seemed to be loving it, as they were hard at work singing away.

When I opened to the door to my place, Duke, my dog, had an alert look on his face. He never made a sound before he knew who was at the door. When he realized it was me, he trotted over to greet me. Duke wasn't a special breed; some would even say he was rather plain looking. He was the last of the Florida Cracker Curs born at my dad's ranch before he decided to start using border collies. I guess I'd felt bad for the pup and decided to keep him. Over time, I had grown attached to him because he was always there at my side. He was like my shadow.

The contrast between the luxury hotel I'd just visited and my home couldn't be any greater. The latter's back door opened to a narrow hall, with my bedroom, kitchen, and bathroom located along one side or the other. The one other room held my tools of the trade. Whether it was PI business or ranch working, my "toolshed," as I called it, had it all; I usually kept it locked. Meanwhile, the hotel had a consistent theme catering to the wealthy. If one had to describe my home's theme, I would say it was mostly country. It depended on my budget and what was available to buy. Most of my furniture was older and acquired from local thrift and antique stores over time.

The other end of the hall opened to an old storefront, which was now my office. This was probably the best part of the building and where I spent most of my tight budget; I figured it was good for business. The ceiling was high so the room would stay cool, just like in the other old buildings. I worked from a large wooden desk with an antique leather chair. I had two more matching chairs in front of the desk for clients. On one side of the room was a glass case mounted on the wall that featured family heirlooms I had managed to hold on to. These were mainly uniform items and weapons used by my family members during the Seminole Wars and the Civil War; most of them had served in the state militia as mounted volunteers or cavalry. I thought the case was a great eye-catcher.

Two large windows faced the street, and the tall, wooden front door also contained a window. The barber next door had introduced me to the handyman who'd painted my business name on the door. It read "Colt Callacy Investigations." Below that was

"Available 24-7 / Will Travel," along with my phone number and website. The handyman had used a Western-style font because of the Western attire I typically wore. He'd also created a matching sign and placed it above the storefront with a light to shine on it all night. I had to admit it looked very nice. I couldn't have been happier.

I looked out the front of the store into the dark to see what was going on in our little town this late at night. The new town hall building was directly across the street and was lit up with floodlights. Between us was a park that was illuminated by street-lights. It stood silent; not one soul was to be found. I often walked through it with Duke during the day when I was trying to gather my thoughts about a case or planning my schedule. A couple of cars were parallel parked in front of the stores next to me. There was hardly any traffic except for a few semitrucks and pickups with horse trailers traveling late into the night.

I closed the blinds and went to work. When I sat down at my desk, I turned on the green banker's lamp in front of me. Duke took note. Once he realized I wasn't going to leave, he went to the bed-room to lie down in his bed. He never liked staying up late.

I started examining the paperwork Chambon had provided me.

"Let's try the obvious first," I said to myself.

I tried calling the transport company—twice. The phone con-tinued to ring without an answer. I couldn't even leave a message. That wasn't necessarily a cause for alarm. It was a small company; maybe they only operated during the day. Their voicemail could have been full, too, typical of some mom-and-pop shops. Unfortu-nately, I was facing a deadline, and that wasn't going to work.

Next, I checked out the quarantine facility on my laptop. It was small and somewhat out of the way from the main airport. I copied the address and brought it up using Google Maps. I took a look at the aerial view.

Not much of a facility, I thought. No hours were listed online. *There might be someone there because of the competition this weekend. They've got to be dealing with other horses.*

I sat back in my desk chair and rubbed my five-o'clock shadow with my right hand. An idea was developing in my head. It was crazy, but it just might work. I leaned forward and looked up the transport company online. There was an old website. They handled other animals, but their specialty was equine transportation. Their home page said they were there to serve the "Horse Capital of the World," as Ocala was known. I looked through the website some more. I needed some pictures.

Jackpot, I thought. Their "About Us" page featured more than enough. The trucks weren't anything special, and the workers did not wear uniforms. They just had clip-on tags hanging from their front shirt pockets. Nothing was uniform. I zoomed in on a picture as best as I could to gather more information.

I stood up from the desk and brought my laptop with me down the hall. Duke took note and hurried in pursuit, something he often did when he thought I was preparing to leave. I pulled out a key from my pocket, unlocked the door to my "toolshed," and turned on the light. When I entered, I placed my laptop down on the table situated along the back wall. Duke came in and curled up in a corner when he realized he had no reason to worry.

I connected my laptop to a large printer I had managed to purchase a year ago. I'd never had a need for it until now. It was just one of those things I'd thought I could use one day. I came up with a quick design using some software on my computer, then compared it to the website. It wasn't exact, but I thought it would pass. When I was confident I had something that wouldn't raise suspicions, I hit print.

The printer went to work creating four copies of the design on magnetic sheets. When the prints were complete, I prepped them for use. I took one and examined it using the fluorescent light from above. Duke picked his head up. He looked puzzled as he gazed at me. I showed him the sign.

"As long as you don't look too close," I said, "no one will notice." Duke walked up to me and sat down at my feet. I looked down at him. "Hopefully no one calls the police. It's a long shot, but it's a starting point."

Duke just cocked his head to one side and stared at the sign.

"IT'S A MODERN-DAY TROJAN HORSE."

The pendulum clock on the wall struck twelve as I exited the toolshed and locked it. Duke was sitting in the back doorway, nervously watching as I put the printed materials in the passenger seat of the truck. The singing critters from earlier had all paused, giving the townsfolk a break from their natural serenade.

I walked back inside and felt the cool air hit me like a wall. I grabbed a plain gray baseball cap I had in my closet. Then I attached the fake identification tag I'd printed to my outer shirt pocket. I gazed in the hallway mirror to take a good look at myself. Then I turned and looked at Duke when he entered.

"What do you think?" I asked. He just stared back at me without moving. He didn't even blink. In a way, he seemed concerned. "Do you want to come?" That's all it took to change his bearing. Duke spun around in a circle like he had some pent-up energy to burn. "You never know. I may need some backup."

Duke and I exited the building, and I locked it. Then I opened the back door to my crew cab truck.

"Jump up!" I said as I tapped the back seat.

Duke shuffled his feet back and forth as he prepped himself for the high jump. Once he was sure, he leaped, landing on the back seat. He ran to the other side of the bench and looked out the window. I took note of his happy face and wagging tail before I shut the door.

With the exception of a couple semitrucks, the streets were vacant, and the storefronts stood dark and silent. I rounded the corner near the water tower and headed toward Carina's; she'd allowed me to keep my horse and trailer at her facility.

Carina was the local vet, and I'd been dating her for a while now. She was a little younger than me and had grown up in the town. She had a marvelous personality. When I was in a bad mood, she was the only one I knew who could change it instantly. It was as if she radiated a special vibe that made you feel welcome. She also loved animals, and they seemed to detect that welcoming aura. From the smallest critters to the largest livestock, they all seemed to be drawn to her and comforted by her presence.

After about a mile, I turned right and entered Carina's facility. It was originally a large farm, with an old ranch-style home up front. It was another one of those old farms that had most of the land sold until it was reduced to a mere ten-acre lot. When Carina's parents had finally retired, they decided to sell the property to her, and she had converted it into a vet clinic to serve the local ranches. I drove down the gravel road that ran along the side of the property line, hoping not to disturb anyone in the main house. Sometimes Carina went to bed early if she had an early house call scheduled. There were a couple of old area lights with metal halide bulbs that emitted a bright green light along the way. When I got to the back of the facility, I circled around and turned on the spotlights hanging from my truck's rear window guard. I backed the truck up, carefully aligning the ball in the truck bed with the gooseneck hitch of my horse trailer. Then I exited the truck and connected it.

My horse, Levi, was in a nearby pen. The dark horse recognized the truck and came trotting to the edge of the fence. I walked over to pet his head and greet him. He was a Cracker horse that I'd bought when I was in my early twenties. I often took him trail riding to keep him in shape, but I had neglected to do so over the past couple weeks. I felt bad because I didn't have a treat to give him.

"I'm sorry, boy," I began. "I don't have anything to give you this time." The poor thing was bored. I could tell he wanted to leave. "Maybe we'll go riding later."

Once he realized he wasn't going anywhere, Levi went back to doing whatever it was he'd been doing.

I walked back to the truck and gathered the magnetic signs I'd printed earlier. I placed two on the back doors of my pickup and two on the sides of the horse trailer. I stepped back and took a good look. Duke was hanging out the window with his tongue dangling from his mouth.

"It's a modern-day Trojan horse," I said out loud with my arms up. I wasn't really talking to anyone; Duke watched, though. I walked back to the truck and had just switched off my spotlights when I heard footsteps behind me. I turned to look.

"Colt?"

It was Carina. It sounded like she had just woken up. She had a small flashlight and was wearing some boots and a bathrobe.

"Colt?" she said again. "What are you doing out here?"

"I'm working late."

"Your truck woke me up. I thought it was another thief."

Carina'd had a utility trailer stolen a couple months ago. I hadn't thought of that until she reminded me.

"I'm sorry, honey." I hugged her to comfort her. "I didn't want to wake you up."

She looked at the signs I'd stuck on my truck and trailer. "What are you up to, Colt?"

"I'm working undercover."

She walked up to the truck. Duke was excited.

"Hey, Dukie," she said. She reached into the window, petted Duke, and pulled out a treat for him from her bathrobe pocket. Then she pointed her flashlight at one of the signs and read it.

"Have you ever heard of that transport company?" I asked.

"No, I've never heard of them. And you're going to get into a lot of trouble doing this."

"What do you mean?"

"You can't go around impersonating a company worker like this." She started walking back toward me.

"According to who?"

"It's against the law. I'm certain of it."

I put my arms around her. Then I looked down at her and smiled. Her green eyes looked back up at me.

"I thought girls liked bad boys."

She pushed me back and smiled. "If you go to jail," she began, continuing to smile, "you can sit there and wait for someone else to get you. I have a busy schedule tomorrow, and I don't have time to bail you out."

"No one is going to know," I said. "And I'm not going to jail."

She pointed toward the highway. She was kind of mad but halfway kidding too.

"Just get out of here. I need to get my sleep. When you're sitting behind bars, you just remember what I said."

I smiled and walked back to the truck. I started the diesel engine and turned on the lights. Carina started walking back between the animal pens, toward her house. I drove back up the gravel road with the trailer squeaking behind me. I stopped once her house was in view and saw her heading up the steps. The red glow of the trailer's brake lights reflected off the side of her house. Carina looked like she was trying to fix her long dark hair as she made her way onto the porch. She looked back, and I tipped my hat toward her with a smile. She smiled and shook her head before disappearing inside.

It took a good hour before I reached the quarantine facility in Marion County. It was located just outside the city limits of Ocala, in a relatively secluded area. I pulled into the facility and stopped to take a look around. The moon offered some light. It looked like a hundred-acre spread, with fenced paddocks situated all around. The gravel road in front of my truck led to a large stable.

"Looks like we're in luck, Duke." The dog turned and looked at me briefly before looking out the front windshield again.

I could see lights on in the stables and some people moving horses into a large three-axle horse trailer. I drove my truck up the path and backed my trailer to the entrance of the stables, just like the other hauler. Duke stood up in his seat when I put the truck in park.

"Stay here," I said. Duke lay down and let out a small cry of displeasure.

I grabbed the paperwork Chambon had provided me and headed toward the entrance of the stables, taking note of the surroundings. It was a clean facility and almost looked new. The nearby fenced corrals looked clean, and the lawns seemed like they were professionally manicured. They were clearly used to handling expensive animals: There were security cameras all around the structure.

When I approached the sliding doors of the stables, two workers leading a horse were walking the opposite way. The older man had gray hair and circles under his eyes. He gave me a puzzled look. He approached me while the younger man kept leading the horse to the trailer.

"Good evening," I said. "Or good morning, I guess I should say."

"Good morning. I'm James. Can we help you?" He seemed baffled to see me.

"I'm here to pick up a mare, Tempest."

"What?" he replied with a surprised look. "She's already been picked up."

I called this tactic playing dumb, but it'd always worked well for me in the past. You could learn a lot of information playing dumb. I just continued to play it cool and pretended like I had no idea what was going on. As far as they knew, I was doing my job—I was just there to pick up a horse for a client.

"What do you mean?" I asked. "Take a look for yourself." I pulled out the paperwork and showed James. "I'm supposed to pick up Tempest and take her to the International Equestrian Park. She's competing this weekend, you know."

He took the file and examined it.

"What company do you work for?" he asked.

I felt kind of bad. He was becoming frustrated trying to figure out what was going on. But I had a job to do. I showed him my fake badge.

"We had a few problems at headquarters today. It's been crazy. I know I'm running late. I'm glad you guys were here. I was worried I wasn't going to be able to get in." I was getting a little nervous. I smiled and tried to pace my speech. If I talked too fast, it might give me away.

"Hold on a minute," he said. He pulled out his phone to make a call. He must have been calling the transport company. Fortunately for me, he had my same luck: No one answered. He put his phone away.

"Look," James said. "There must be a mix-up. Tempest was picked up earlier. They even signed for her. Come with me to the office. I'll show you."

I followed him inside the stables. Lights from above lit the entire structure, making it very easy to see. All the horses were being nosey. They were hanging their heads out of the stalls, examining all the commotion happening so early in the morning. A couple shook their heads up and down as we passed.

We went around an old work truck parked inside and arrived at the office located in the middle of the building.

"Have a seat," James said. He waved me toward a chair in front of the desk. I sat down as he walked behind the desk and began searching through a metal filing cabinet. Next to the cabinet were a couple of old monitors for the security system.

"Here it is." He opened a file and laid it in front of me. "She was picked up around four this afternoon. I hope you know this person. I'm going to call the police if you don't."

I'd just started looking at the paperwork when someone yelled out from the entrance.

"James! I need your help."

James looked out the door of the office, then back at me. He hesitated for a minute. I looked at him the best I could with my peripheral vision. I could tell he didn't want to leave me alone.

He finally gave in. "I'm coming!" Turning to me, he said, "I'll be right back." James exited the room at a fast pace.

Once I was certain he was gone, I pulled my phone out and began taking pictures of the paperwork. I didn't have time to examine everything in detail. I had to move fast. Once I had the file copied, I walked over to the door and looked out over the stalls. James wasn't in sight. I hurried back inside and started examining the monitors.

Perfect, I thought to myself. The surveillance system was old and easy to figure out. It didn't require a password, either. I played back the footage to around 3:50 p.m. and looked over my shoulder to make sure the coast was clear. Then I started fast-forwarding through the footage.

At 3:58 p.m., a truck and large horse trailer backed up to the entrance of the stables. The driver exited the cab and appeared to be talking with another worker in the passenger seat. James greeted the driver, and they both went inside. At about 4:02 p.m., the driver walked back to the truck and handed the paperwork to the passenger. Another couple minutes went by before the passenger returned the paperwork to the driver. The driver then headed back inside the stables. He and James returned with Tempest and loaded her into the trailer, and the truck left after James shook hands with the driver.

I backed up the footage again and snapped pictures of the truck, trailer, and tag on the back of the trailer.

"I'll be right there," James yelled. He was making his way back to the office. I put the monitors back to record and hurried to my seat. I put my phone to my ear. James saw the phone and entered quietly. He walked over and sat down in the chair behind the desk. Then he leaned back and folded his hands on his chest. I pulled the phone from my ear and put it down.

"I don't know what happened," I said. I shook my head like I was in disbelief. "I can't get anyone to answer. They had to have given me the wrong paperwork or something."

I stood up and handed him the file. He leaned forward in the chair and took it. I shook his hand and gathered my paperwork and phone. "I'm sorry for the disruption. You guys look very busy tonight."

"It's alright." James seemed a little more relaxed now that the mix-up was taken care of. "It happens sometimes. When these big shows occur at the park, the whole city seems to be in a rush. We're thankful for the business, but I can't wait for it to be over. I want to get some sleep."

I laughed lightly.

"Thanks for everything," I said. I reached out and shook his hand.

"Glad to help," James replied. "Have a safe night."

~ 4 ~

"YOU'RE LUCKY WE'RE CLOSE FRIENDS."

The night had given way to an alternate world seen by few. Uniform retail stores, normally busy with a rush of customers, had been replaced by stock crews hard at work packing the shelves for the next day. Tractor-trailers lined the backs of the stores as they dropped off their loads. The parking lots were lit with LED streetlights and served as rest areas where eighteen-wheelers and campers parked to get a couple hours of sleep. Street sweepers with flashing yellow caution lights passed around the parked vehicles, attempting to clean the lots as best they could before the break of dawn.

When I was certain I was a safe distance from the facility, I entered the parking lot of a tractor dealership and parked my truck. I exited and took a look around. I was just on the outskirts of Ocala. The area was normally full of people during the day, and I wanted to make sure no one was watching. I needed to remove the signs from my truck and trailer before I got in trouble.

Once I was satisfied we were alone, I began removing the fake advertisements. Duke watched me carefully as I pulled each sign off one by one, dried them off from the damp night air, and stacked them neatly under the back seat, out of sight. With the signs gone, I figured it would be okay if I parked here for a little while longer. If an officer stopped and asked, I would just explain that I was taking a break from driving like the truckers and campers across the street.

I leaned against the brush guard to stretch my legs and pulled out my phone to examine the pictures I'd taken earlier. I glanced behind me to check on Duke. He continued to keep a careful eye on me. He had the look of a determined cattle dog. I went back to probing the pictures. I examined the truck and trailer from the surveillance footage. At one point, I could see both figures in the truck before they backed the trailer to the entrance. I tried to zoom in for a closer look. I was curious as to who the passenger was, but I couldn't make them out. The photo was too blurry. I was just wasting time.

I looked at the next photograph on my phone. It was a close-up of the tag on the back of the trailer. I headed back around, stepped up into the cab of my truck, and sat down with the door open. I opened the center console and began looking for something to write with. I found a pen and wrote down the tag number on the manila file holding Chambon's paperwork. It was a new lead, but I was going to need some help before I could follow it. I pulled out my phone and gave Will a call.

William "Will" Autry was a deputy sheriff in Levy County and a close friend. When my father and I had had some differences and I'd left home, I'd enlisted in the Florida National Guard since I had no other place to go. That was where I met Will. We went through boot camp and practically served together. We always had each other's backs. Will was also the person who first familiarized me with Williston. He'd grown up there and always had good things to say about the small town. He once invited me to see Williston for myself, and I never left after that.

We eventually went our own ways. Will went to the police academy and ended up working in Bronson, and I earned my private investigator license and worked different jobs until I could afford to set up shop in Williston.

I felt bad for what I was about to do. If it weren't for Will, I wouldn't have ever found Williston or met Carina. God only knew where I would have ended up.

I waited a few minutes as the phone rang. It was early, but he often worked the night shift. There was finally an answer.

"Will, it's Colt."

"Colt? Everything alright?"

"Everything is fine. You off tonight?"

"No, I'm working late again. New guy on the block. You know how it goes." He paused. "What are you up to?"

"I'm working on another case. I could really use some help."

"What do you need?"

"Remember when you said you owed me a favor?"

"Yes, I remember." Will was hesitant with his reply. I could tell he wasn't sure about what was coming next.

"You think you could run a plate for me?"

"Colt," he started, "you know I shouldn't be doing that."

"Come on. I'm in a bind. I have a good client, and I'm pressed for time."

"Colt..."

"Will, you owe me a big favor. Remember how I helped you?" I had helped Will with another case. We'd had a couple guys going around stealing utility trailers from local farms, probably the same ones who'd taken Carina's trailer. I'd staked out a couple farms over the course of three weeks to help Will track down the culprits. It helped him out at work, and I never asked for pay. I was just helping an old friend. Still, there was silence on the other end of the phone.

"Will, you there?"

"I'm here." There was another pause. "I'll do it this one time, but I can't be using the department's resources like this in the future. I don't want to lose my job. I've got a good career going here."

"I won't ask again. Promise." I supplied Will with the plate number.

"You're lucky we're close friends. And don't you dare tell anybody about this. I mean anybody."

"This conversation never even happened."

"Just hold on a minute."

A few minutes went by before Will spoke again. "The trailer is registered to a farm in Lake County. It's just outside of Eustis." He gave me the address. "Is that it?"

"That's all I need. Thanks, Will. I appreciate it."

"That's it. Okay. We're even now. That was a huge favor."

"We're even. Promise. I won't ask again."

"Take care of yourself, alright."

"You do the same."

We ended the conversation, and I entered the address into my phone. We were about an hour away from the residence. I shut the door to the truck and started the engine.

I looked over my shoulder at Duke. "Well, we've got another lead."

Duke looked at me and then out the window as if he were curious as to where we were heading next.

~ 5 ~

"THAT DAMN DOG."

As we crossed into the next county, the nightlife of Ocala faded, giving way to lakes glittering in the moonlight. On turning north of Eustis, the scene changed again to tranquil groves of oaks, pines, and palms. The occasional clearing appeared, giving way to a small farm lit by an old metallic area light attached to a post or the eve of a barn. The road ahead lay quiet in the headlights, interrupted only by the odd herd of deer grazing alongside the road or a passing car heading in the opposite direction.

It had taken us a little over an hour to reach the address. Duke had decided to curl up in the back seat and go to sleep shortly after we'd left the parking lot of the dealership. He was a creature of habit and often went to bed at about half past ten each night. How? I had no idea. It was like he had an internal clock. Either way, he slept for most of the trip, at least until my phone told me to turn off the county highway and onto a gravel road. I turned on my blinker and brought the truck to a slow crawl before slightly veering into the other lane to make the large turn with the trailer. Duke sat up out of a dead sleep to see what was happening.

The gravel road was rough and appeared to be washed out in a couple areas. I slowed the speed of the pickup so the gravel wouldn't fly off the tires and scratch the paint on the truck or the trailer. I just took my time. It was completely dark. Once in a while, a double-wide home or an old worn-down farmhouse with a barn would peek out of the woods.

I looked in the rearview mirror. Duke was constantly switching between looking out the front windshield and the rear passenger windows. It seemed like he was trying to get his bearings.

This is going to be tricky, I thought to myself. I peered out the windshield and side windows. I had one hand on the steering wheel and the other arm resting on the center console. Duke glanced at me with a puzzled look before returning to peering out the windows.

In my experience, neighbors out here were close and often watched out for one another. They were suspicious of anything out of the norm, and many were armed for self-protection. People out here also tended to wake up early in the morning. I had already seen a few lights on in some of the homes. The best-case scenario would be for me to leave before daybreak to avoid any trouble.

When the phone said I was about a mile from the address, I slowed the truck some more and rolled down the windows. I could hear gravel crunching under the treads of the tires. The running lights reflected off the trees lining both sides of the road. I opened my door, leaned out with one foot on the running board, and examined the road ahead. Satisfied with what I saw, I sat back in the truck and closed the door.

"I think we have enough room, Duke."

I turned the truck wide and attempted to make a U-turn with the trailer. The sound of the diesel engine intensified and the exhaust whistled as I pressed the accelerator with the load of the trailer behind me. I was close to completing the turn, but one small pine tree was in my way. I put the truck in reverse and turned the wheels in the opposite direction to take another jab. The engine got loud again, and the truck slowly moved, repositioning the front of the trailer. I drove forward again, this time clearing the tree. As I straightened the truck and trailer, a set of headlights appeared in my side mirror.

Damn it, I thought to myself. I drove my rig to the side of the road and put it in park.

The headlights were just behind my trailer and closing in. I was ready with an excuse in case he stopped. I'd seen a town nearby on my phone's map. It was called Umatilla. I was going to explain that I was lost and trying to find the best way back to that town—it was all I could think of. The headlights were now slowly creeping up alongside my rig. The beams finally passed my mirrors, revealing an old dark truck with a bed cap. The driver was a heavy older man with a beard; he was sporting a baseball cap. As he passed my truck cab, he slowed down some more and gave me a stern look. He didn't seem to appreciate my presence. Luckily, he sped up and drove right on by. Maybe he just wanted to be left alone.

Once the old man was out of sight, I turned off the headlights and shut off the engine. Then I exited the cab. I took a look around in the dark. I didn't see any homes nearby. I looked up at the sky. I could just see the faint orange light of dawn approaching. I reached back into the truck, grabbed my binoculars from the glove box, and attached their case to my belt.

"Stay here and watch the truck," I told Duke. "And please be quiet."

It was as if he understood me perfectly. He sat down and assumed a strict posture. He started looking about in all directions like a guard on duty. I shut the door and headed to the trailer. I opened the side door to the tack compartment, grabbed a halter, rope, and a pair of wire cutters. During my drive, I noticed most of the farms out here were fenced with barbed wire. I doubted where I was heading was any different. Then I shut the door and started heading toward the address.

I used the dim light of my phone screen to light the way. It wasn't as bright as a flashlight, and I thought it concealed my position better. I tried to stay off to the side of the road so the gravel wouldn't make any noise under my cowboy boots. I saw a metal mailbox appear in front of me. Beside it was a muddy road that led deeper into the woods. I looked at the house number on the box and compared it to the address on my phone. It was the address that Will had given me.

I started making my way down the road but stayed just off the side, using the woods as cover. The walk was rough. Some areas had standing water, and the mud made it feel like my boots were being sucked off my feet, but I managed. After about ten minutes, the woods gave way to another clearing. I ducked down and made my way as close to the clearing as possible, using some tall grass and short sabal palms as cover. Then I pulled my binoculars out to take a good look at the clearing.

The sun had yet to fully rise, but it offered just enough light to get a good look at the property. There was a mobile home with a powerline running to the roof. A small shack, probably a well house, stood next to it. Behind it was a barn with the doors wide open. I could see the truck from the surveillance footage parked inside. Muddy roads surrounded all the structures. Behind everything were fenced fields. There were no lights on in the double-wide. Everything seemed to be quiet.

I slowly headed deeper into the woods. Then I made my way around the farm. I tried to be as quiet as possible so as not to wake anyone. Once I'd circled around the main structures, I walked toward the fence and hid behind an oak tree surrounded by tall grass. I pulled the binoculars out again and took a look. There was one dark horse grazing in the field, next to a lone palm tree. I looked over at the double-wide. The lights were still out. The coast was clear. I stepped out into the clearing to take a better look. The horse saw me and decided to wander up. It probably thought it was time to eat.

As the animal got closer, I was able to get a better look at it. A black mare was making her way toward the fence. When she got close enough, I pet her muzzle to calm her and show her she had nothing to worry about. She seemed to be well tamed. I ran my hands down her right leg; she wasn't bothered by the motion. I found what I was looking for: the scar that Mrs. Philippe had cited. There was no doubt that this was Tempest.

"Let's get you out of here, Tempest," I said. "I bet you're ready to get back to Mrs. Philippe." Tempest turned her head slightly when she heard her name.

She was already wearing a halter, so I attached the rope to it as a lead so she wouldn't wander off. I was worried about how she would react at first, but she seemed fine. It made sense, I guess. Tempest must have become acquainted with being handled by strangers; after all, she had been flown all around the world as a competing show jumper. Not that I knew anything about this type of horse.

My intuition regarding the fence was correct. It was barbed wire. It was a cheap and effective solution for fencing animals. However, this must have been a temporary stop for Tempest—barbed wire was usually never used to fence horses. This field had more likely been designed to confine cattle.

Once I had a firm grasp on the rope, I took the wire cutters and began cutting each strand of barbed wire. Tempest was watching carefully. Maybe she was ready to leave, too. I started at the top. The wire popped from the tension, and both sides of the cut wire swung at me before drooping down. I pulled the loose ends back and wrapped the wire around the other sections of the fence. Then I repeated the process. When the final wire popped open, one barb caught on my jeans. I carefully removed it and wrapped it around the other side of the fence.

Once I was certain it was okay for Tempest to pass, I grabbed the rope with my right hand and tried to reduce the slack as much as possible. I carried the excess rope, halter, and cutters in my left hand and gave the rope a quick tug with my right. Tempest complied with the demand and followed.

The wet ground muffled some of the noise from Tempest's hooves, but I wouldn't be able to disappear into the woods like before. There was too much brush for the large purebred to pass through. We would have to stay in the clearing and walk down the driveway to get to the gravel road. We slowly made our way toward the exit along the outside perimeter of the fence, careful not to make any noise that would raise suspicion. It was hard. It seemed like every step we took was amplified. We paused, and I looked over at the double-wide. The lights were still out, and there was no sign of movement.

"We might be in luck, Tempest," I said. Tempest didn't do anything. "Come on." I gave the rope another tug, and she followed. I took one more look back at the house. It was still quiet. "We just might get away with this."

No sooner had I said that when a horrifying sound hit my ears. My phone started ringing! I'd forgotten to put it on silent. It had to be the transport company. I hadn't even left a message for them to return my call. I couldn't believe it. I panicked!

I started fumbling with my pocket, trying to get the phone out. Tempest's ears perked up as it continued to ring. When I finally got it out, it slipped from my grasp and hit the ground. The phone continued ringing. I scrambled to pick it up off the ground. Then I fumbled it in my hands, trying to determine which side was right side up. Once it was upright, I felt around for the volume button and turned it down. Then I put it back in my pocket.

I looked over at the double-wide again; a light was on in one of the rooms now. I tugged the rope and hurried Tempest down the muddy road until we were out of sight. I began to worry. They wouldn't be too far behind. They were going to be ticked once they saw that I'd cut their fence, let alone walked onto their property without permission and taken Tempest. We needed to move fast!

I thought about what to do next. Then, an idea hit me. I'd seen it in some old Westerns. I'd never tried it myself, but now was as good a time as any.

"Alright, Tempest. I know I'm a stranger, but I need you to trust me."

I took the rope, made makeshift reins, and placed them around her neck. She didn't run. She seemed okay with it. Next was the moment of truth. I stepped back to get a running start and kept the reins in my left hand. I took a deep breath and leaped up, hoping to slide on top of Tempest. She shifted quickly, and I didn't land directly on top of her back. She panicked for a second or two and started bucking. I fought to keep myself from sliding off. When I was finally upright, she calmed.

"Walk on," I said. Tempest began to walk. After a few seconds, I had a feel for riding bareback, so I popped my legs and put on some pressure. Tempest began to hurry down the road. I looked behind me. No one was in sight.

When we reached the end of the driveway, I pulled the reins to the right and popped my legs again, making Tempest move faster. All the while, I was fighting to stay on top of her. The sun was beginning to appear on the horizon. We were running out of time.

A walk that had seemed to take forever before was cut down to seconds on horseback. When we got to my rig, I quickly slid off Tempest, opened the back doors to the trailer, and began to lead her inside. She hesitated. I figured the commotion of everything had scared her, but I didn't have time. I moved my hand up the rope and started petting her snout, reassuring her that everything was alright. As I calmed her, I kept looking down the road, waiting for someone to emerge from the driveway. Finally, Tempest got comfortable enough to follow me into the trailer. I led her directly toward the front and tied her off to one of the metal rings on the wall. She started looking out the window as I closed and secured the divider. Then I hurried out the back of the trailer and shut the doors.

I took a quick look down the road. Still no sign of anyone. I hurried back toward the truck. It was basically daytime now. I opened the cab, jumped in, and threw the wire cutters and extra halter on the floor. I'd been so worked up I'd forgot I was carrying them. Duke was still on guard and knew something was up. He started running back and forth between the rear side windows. I started the truck and gunned it. I looked in my rearview mirror but didn't see any cars.

The quiet hobby farms I had passed earlier were now full of life. People were getting ready to go to work and start their daily routines. Many paused and watched the unfamiliar truck and trailer that sped by, kicking up gravel and dust.

The commotion was too much for Duke. He couldn't help it. He hung his head out the window, tail straight up, and started barking at the neighbors who were staring at us.

"Duke!" I yelled.

He continued to bark.

"Duke! Be quiet! I see them, Duke! Please stop!"

It was no use. Duke continued to draw more attention to us. I felt like the driver of a traveling circus. It seemed like every person in that part of the county wanted to get a good look at us as we passed by. I just floored it. What else could I do?

When we reached the end of the gravel road, I slowed down just enough to check for traffic on the highway. I didn't see any in either direction. Without even stopping, I turned the corner sharply and gunned it again. I looked in the rearview mirror to check the load. In the back seat, Duke swayed on all fours with the motion of the vehicle, tongue hanging out and a happy look on his face. He appeared to be having the time of his life.

That damn dog, I thought to myself.

~ 6 ~

"IT'S MORE LIKE A GAME OF POKER."

The morning sun was rising high in the sky. The damp blanket of dew that had coated the landscape throughout the night was dissipating as the temperature climbed. Steam radiated from the asphalt as the truck cruised out of Lake County and into Marion County. The nightlife of Ocala had been replaced with heavy stop-and-go traffic as people went to work and ran errands. West of the city, however, was easy going.

I had the diesel purring at a constant speed of sixty-five miles an hour once I was west of I-75. I glanced in the rearview mirror to check on everything. Duke was out cold in the back seat. He must've been worn out from his earlier hell-raising. He was lying on his side, and his body was moving slightly with the motion of the truck. I smiled and kept quiet so as not to disturb him.

Thirty more minutes went by before Williston's water tower came into view. I was excited. I couldn't believe that not only had I tracked down Tempest so quickly, but we'd also gotten away without running into anyone. I rounded the curve back into Williston and slowed down a bit before crossing the railroad tracks. A thud hit each of the tires of the truck as they rolled over the rails. A second went by, and the trailer jerked, letting me know it had cleared the tracks. The sound was reassuring. It had been a successful trip. I had Tempest, I was home, and I was ready to wrap up this case and get paid.

Traffic had picked up some in my small town. Still, it only took a couple minutes to pass through the main strip. A typical busy day. I made the turn near the water tower and began heading south toward Carina's. I turned again and entered her facility. The trailer squeaked and jumped around as I made my way down the gravel road. Everything seemed wet from the dew. At the end of the road, I circled around, then put the truck in reverse and backed the trailer near an empty pen next to Levi's. After parking my rig, I exited the truck and then opened the back door of the cab.

"Come on, Duke," I said. "Stretch your legs."

Duke dove out of the truck and ran up to Levi to check on him. He put his front paws on the steel corral panel to get closer to him. Levi stretched his neck over the fence and hung his head down to see Duke.

I walked over to the window on the trailer and opened it. I left the bars closed just in case Tempest tried to exit through the small opening.

"How was your trip?" I asked. Tempest looked around at the new scenery. Then I heard some stomping coming from the trailer. She was ready to get out. "Alright, I'm coming, Tempest. Just wait another minute."

I opened the gate to the empty pen and then opened the trailer doors. Everything seemed okay back there. I opened the divider and stayed clear of Tempest's back end in case she decided to kick or back out of the trailer. I untied the rope from the metal ring and began backing her out. She seemed fine with this. It obviously wasn't the first time she'd been trailered. At the edge of the trailer, she slowly found her footing as she stepped down to the ground. Once she was clear of the trailer, I led her into the pen and closed the gate, removing the rope and halter so that she would be more comfortable. Then I climbed over the fence to exit.

Tempest paused, then moved her head around to take in her surroundings. Levi instantly took an interest in her and headed to the side of his pen to get a closer look. Tempest glanced at him for a minute, then spun around in the opposite direction before gracefully walking around the perimeter of her pen. Was she checking out her pen or playing hard to get?

"Forget it Levi," I said. "She's out of your league. She's from high society. She might be playing with you."

I headed over to a nearby shed and grabbed a couple buckets of feed. I gave one to Levi and the other to Tempest. Then I filled their troughs with fresh water. Levi started eating, while Tempest took a few sips of water. While they ate, I cleaned out the trailer, parked it in its usual spot, and unhitched it.

All the commotion finally drew Carina's attention. She was wearing jeans, boots, a T-shirt, and a baseball cap. Her dark hair was in a ponytail. I could see her skinny, fit figure swaying as she made her way over from the main house. I had to admit, her walk perked my interest. Duke went running up to her and rolled over in front of her feet, stopping her progress. She bent down and rubbed his stomach.

"Hey, Dukie," she said. Duke lay there with a small portion of his tongue just hanging out of his mouth. Carina stood up and gave him a treat. Duke ate it and starting running in circles around her as she approached me.

"What is this?" she demanded as she walked up and pointed at Tempest.

"This is Tempest," I replied.

"I'm not taking in another one of your horses," she said. She placed her hands on her hips. "You're lucky I let Levi stay here."

"It's only temporary. I had to track her down. She was stolen."

"Stolen? What happened?"

"Don't know. Someone picked her up from quarantine."

"Quarantine? Where's she from?"

"France. She's a show jumper."

Carina walked up to the pen and took a closer look at Tempest. The mare walked up to her, and Carina pet her nose. She reached into her pocket and presented Tempest with a treat.

"She looks like an excellent breed," Carina said. "I can see she's been well taken care of."

"My client is waiting for her. She's at the International Equestrian Park."

"Then why is your trailer unhitched?" Carina wanted answers. "Why aren't you taking Tempest there? I need this pen."

"I just want to make sure I get paid."

"Colt, I can tell from the horse that these people have money. I'm sure you're going to be paid."

"I have all kinds of people conveniently forget to pay me. Some rich, even. At least they appear to be."

"This sounds like a ransom."

"It's more like a game of poker. Think of it like calling someone's bluff."

"Colt, why don't you get a better line of work?"

"I'm going to get her out of here, I promise. Besides, she's warming up to you."

"She seems to have a very sweet personality." Carina continued to stroke Tempest's muzzle.

"Look," I said, "even Levi likes her. He has a new girlfriend." Levi's attention had left the food, and he'd started staring at Tempest again.

"At least he's hanging with a better class of woman." Carina paused. "Why do I put up with you and your horse?"

I walked over and embraced her. She stopped petting Tempest and looked up at me. "Because I kind of like you. I kind of like you a lot." She smiled. "I promise it's only temporary. Let me run back to my place and make a call. I'll have her out of here today."

Carina looked over at Tempest, then back at me.

"She'll be gone by the end of the day?" she asked, seeking reassurance.

"By the end of the day," I replied. "Promise."

"I'm going to hold you to that." Carina turned and started to head back to the house. Then she stopped and turned back. "Take a good look at what you'll be missing if you don't." Carina spun back around. I watched her as her cute figure swayed back and forth. She turned her head to the right slightly, just enough to ensure I was eyeing her as she walked back.

Oh, she's good, I thought.

Once she was out of view, I turned and headed to the truck. I opened the back door and patted the back seat twice.

"Hurry up, Duke," I said. "We've got to get that horse outta here."

Duke looked at me, got a running start, and leaped into the back of the truck, happily ready for another ride. I slammed the door shut and hurried into the cab. Within a few seconds, I had the truck barreling back up the gravel road and toward home.

I entered the back door of my place, and Duke followed. It was starting to get warm from the summer sun, so I turned the AC down a couple degrees. Duke went to his bed, circled a couple times, then dropped into place with a loud thud. He had to be beat. I headed down the hall and into the open area of my office. I put on some coffee and opened the wooden blinds to let the light in. Drivers sped by my office in intervals with the changing of the stoplight at the corner.

I sat down at my desk and listened to the coffee percolate and the sounds of traffic as I began searching through my phone for Mrs. Philippe's number. I had a few tabs open and scrolled through each, closing them one by one. When I came upon the pictures of the paperwork from the facility, something caught my attention: a large cursive *C* at the beginning of a signature. I clicked the picture, expanded it, and took a closer look. Then I compared it to one of Chambon's signatures in the paperwork he'd provided me with. There was no doubt that the signature belonged to him. I sat back in my chair and paused for a minute, wondering what to do next.

I took a chance and called the facility. I waited a few minutes for an answer.

"Hello," I heard on the other end.

"Good morning. Is James available?"

"This his him."

"James, I'm the one who showed up last night regarding Tempest."

"Right. Did you get everything straightened out? I think your company called me, but I haven't replied back yet."

"I think so. I just had a question about the paperwork."

"Of course."

"I saw a signature for Mr. Chambon. How did—"

"That's correct."

"Was he there yesterday afternoon?"

There was a pause on the other end of the line.

"I was in a hurry," James began. He seemed a little worried now. "I didn't meet him personally. He stayed in the truck. I worked with the driver only. He relayed the information to Chambon in the truck, and he signed everything there. I took the driver at his word. Is everything okay? I was just getting overwhelmed here, and I cut some corners. God, I hope I don't lose my job!"

"Calm down," I said. I felt bad for him. I made up a quick excuse. "You're fine. I just wanted to make sure we had everything we needed. Your secret is safe with me."

We said our goodbyes and hung up. I opened my laptop and did a raw search for Chambon and Mrs. Philippe. I used their full names. The computer pulled me deeper into its virtual world, and I lost track of my surroundings. I wanted to know what was going on now. Chambon had to be playing me.

I searched for several minutes, but nothing came up on Chambon. I found a couple of old addresses in New Orleans, but those could have been for people with similar names. It was like he didn't exist. Mrs. Philippe came up a few times, mainly because of her former husband's endeavors as a philanthropist. His funeral had been very large and received some media attention back in France.

The tie between the World Wide Web and me was quickly severed by reality when my phone rang. It was Carina.

"Babe, what's wrong?"

"You need to come quick!" She sounded frantic.

"What's wrong? Are you okay? Is someone bothering you?" I was worried someone had followed me to her place and was giving her a hard time over Tempest.

"No, it's Tempest! There's something wrong with her!"

"I'll be right there!"

I hung up the phone, slipped it into my pocket, grabbed my Stetson, and hurried out the back door with Duke trailing behind me.

~ 7 ~

"I'M NOT READY TO SHOW MY HAND JUST YET."

A trip that normally took a few minutes felt like it was reduced to mere seconds. We bolted down the gravel road of Carina's place, then circled back near the pens. The sun had baked the countryside just enough to dry out the road's surface. A trail of dust now streamed from the truck tires along the way.

I swung the truck around on the gravel, held on to the steering wheel with both hands, and slammed the brakes. The truck skidded a few feet on the gravel before coming to a complete stop. Duke struggled to keep his balance in the back seat and fell forward as we stopped. I swung open my door; Duke jumped from the back seat to the front and followed me out of the cab. He knew something was up, and he wanted to be right there at my side. At this point, the trailing dust had caught up with us and engulfed both us and the truck.

The dust blocked my view momentarily, but I heard something surreal. It sounded horselike, but it was a cross between a long neigh and a deep scream. The odd sound then gave way to moaning. When I found my way out of the dust cloud, I saw Carina leaning against the fence enclosing Tempest. She was in tears.

Tempest was in pain. Carina couldn't stand the sight of any animal suffering. Nor could I. The mare was slowly walking in circles in her pen. Her breathing was heavy and seemed to be slow-paced. A few more seconds went by before she found a burst of energy.

She began jumping back and forth and shaking her head violently. It was like she was trying to shake something off. She was fighting something, for sure. After a few more seconds, she returned to walking in circles.

As Tempest passed by, I took a closer look. I leaned on the fence and reached out to touch her muzzle when she came close, but Carina grabbed my arm and pulled it back.

"Don't touch her," she said. "I don't know how she's going to react."

"What the hell happened?" I asked.

"I don't know. I was making my rounds and checking on the animals. She was fine one minute, and then she started that weird noise and began shaking her head."

"Have you ever seen this before?"

"Never."

Tempest circled around again. I tried to lean in for a closer look.

"Colt, please be careful. God only knows what's wrong with that poor thing."

"Look at her eyes," I said. "They don't look right."

Tempest's pace was slowing, and her head was drooping. She looked like she was fighting to stay awake. She continued to walk the perimeter of the fence. When she came near again, Carina leaned forward to take a closer look for herself.

"Her pupils," she said. "They're very thin."

Tempest turned away from the fence and started making her way toward the center of the pen. She appeared to be choking or gurgling. Levi watched from his pen. His ears pointed in the direction of Tempest. He was curious about all the commotion. Duke walked up to the fence and put his front paws on the bottom rail. He seemed to be worried about Tempest, too. The mare slowly walked some more before coming to a complete stop. Her breathing was very heavy and even slower at this point.

"Oh, no!" said Carina.

Tempest started to sway some before falling on her side. Forgetting about what she'd just said to me, Carina jumped the metal fence panel and went running up to her. I was trailing behind her, struggling to keep up in my boots. Tempest picked her head up, and her legs moved some. It was like the mare was in denial of what was happening to her. Carina knelt down and began rubbing her muzzle. I knelt down beside them both.

"Calm down," Carina said softly. She continued to rub Tempest. "Just relax."

Tempest unclenched her legs. Carina adjusted her position and sat down. Tempest laid her head in Carina's lap. I figured she was looking for any kind of comfort at that point. The mare seemed to be gazing at something in the distance. A couple minutes went by before she breathed in deeply and then exhaled her last breath.

"She's gone," said Carina. She had the sniffles, and she was rubbing some tears from her eyes. "I always hate to see this." She hugged Tempest's muzzle before I helped move the mare's head from her lap so she could get up.

"Colt, what the hell happened? Where did you get this horse?"

"She was stolen. The owner hired me to track her down. I found her last night."

Carina rubbed her face and gathered herself. "Where did you say this horse came from earlier?"

"France."

"So, she was shipped into the country recently?"

"Yes, just a few days ago."

Carina paused and thought about it. "I'll be right back," she said.

She climbed over the fence and headed toward the house. I started to examine Tempest up close. Duke walked up to her muzzle, smelled her, and began poking her with his paw like he was hoping she would get up.

"Stop, Duke," I said. "She's not going to get up."

Duke lay down and began staring at her. It was like he was still hoping she would get up.

I looked a little closer at her muzzle. Then I noticed that her lips were blue. Carina broke my concentration when she reappeared, carrying a couple of bags. She had an angry look on her face.

"Colt, take this." I walked over to the fence and grabbed the two bags. I pulled them through the rails. Then Carina climbed back over.

"What is this?"

"It's a portable ultrasound."

"What's wrong?"

"I want to check her intestines. Do you see her mouth?"

"I looked at her lips. They're blue."

"That means her lips were not receiving oxygen. I have an idea of what might be going on. I hope I'm wrong."

Carina began unpacking the bags and preparing the ultrasound. This was another side of her that I found attractive. When she was determined to accomplish something, she did it. She never gave up. This was her element. Her career was more than a job. It was her passion. When something was wrong with one of her patients, she wanted to get to the bottom of it.

She began rubbing ultrasound gel on Tempest.

"Hold this," Carina said. She was very serious. She handed me the monitor. I held it so she could watch the screen while she moved the probe. Her eyes were as sharp as those of an eagle looking for its prey. "There it is."

"There's what?"

"Take a look."

I turned the monitor and took a glance. Her intestines contained what looked like a small package.

"She's a drug mule?" I asked.

"It looks like it," Carina replied. "I'm not going to know for sure until I remove it. I need to get in there."

I helped Carina pick up the portable ultrasound and put Duke in the house before we prepared for the autopsy. The procedure took a while, and I aided her during the entire process. She was dressed in a surgical gown, rubber gloves, and a faceguard. It was different seeing her like this. I'd always known about her work, but I'd never really seen her in action. She had the precision of a surgeon you might see on one of those medical shows. I helped her by providing her tools when she requested them.

"There it is," she said. I looked over and saw a small, clear plastic package in the horse's intestines. Carina stood up and started working it out, careful not to break it.

She stood up and handed me the bag. I began examining it with the rubber gloves she'd had me wear. There was a white powdery substance packed tight inside.

"Here's another one," Carina said. She kept pulling bags out. "And here's the culprit. Bastards! Sick bastards! Look." She showed me the final bag. It had ruptured. "Poor thing! I hate people who treat animals like this."

She stood up, paused, and took a deep breath. "I've heard of this before, in the exotic animal trade. They managed to get Tempest to swallow these packages. Then they probably gave her antimotility drugs to slow her digestion. Once Tempest arrived, they were probably going to wait for the process to be completed so they could get the drugs back."

"Are there any more?"

Carina probed around one final time. "I don't see anything else, Colt. It looks like it's four altogether. How did you find these people?"

"I don't know." I shrugged. "Just my luck, I guess." I took another look at the bags. "Is there any way we can test them to see what this is?"

Carina looked at Tempest, then back at me. "Since the bag ruptured, she ingested it. The contents made it into her bloodstream. I will need to do a blood test to find out."

"How long will it take?"

"I can run the test here on-site," she replied. "I'm not sure how long it will take me, though. I'm not sure what I'm looking for."

I helped Carina clean up her instruments, and we took the bags to the clinic, which was located in a building next to the main house. It sat behind a small gravel parking lot near the main road. Her lab was located in the back. Luckily, the vet office was closed, though Carina was always on standby in case of an emergency. She went right to work running the test.

It took about an hour before she had the results. I was sitting down in a chair in the empty waiting area, reviewing the case in my head. Carina finally broke my train of thought when she exited her lab.

"It's carfentanil."

"Are you sure?" I asked.

"Certain."

"That's a rare drug. The street value there has got to be through the roof. I don't ever remember dealing with it in the National Guard."

"It's extremely potent, too," she said. "Vets use this to tranquilize large animals like elephants. A small trace at the end of a pencil could be lethal. We've got to be careful when we handle these packages."

"That makes sense. I can't see anyone going through all this trouble for cocaine. This is worth their while."

"Colt, I really think we should call the police now."

I thought about the situation and rubbed my chin. Then I stood up, walked into the lab, and began sorting through the packages.

"I'll give Will a call in a minute."

"What are you doing?"

"Remember when I told you about playing poker earlier?"

"Yes?" she said with an unsure look. "What are you fixing to do?"

"I'm not ready to show my hand just yet."

~ 8 ~

"PROMISE."

The high noon summer sun barreled down on the facility, causing the temperature to rise, along with the humidity. The shock of the episode earlier had given way to a state of curiosity and perhaps a slight feeling of fear.

"I may need some leverage if I'm going to figure this thing out," I said. "Plus, you never know what to expect from these guys ... in my experience."

"Colt, all you're going to figure out is why girls are smarter. You're going to end up thinking back on what I just said. Please just call Will and turn everything over to him."

"I'm going to. I just need a few more minutes."

Carina placed the ruptured bag in another bag and sealed it tight. I picked it up, along with one of the full bags.

"Colt, what are you doing?" Carina followed behind me as I started searching around the room.

"Where is a good place to secure these bags until Will arrives? Just to keep them out of sight."

"We'll lock everything in the drug cabinet." She grabbed her key and opened the cabinet, and I placed the two bags inside. Then I grabbed the remaining two bags and started to head out the back exit.

"Where are you going?"

"It's just in case."

"Colt, please don't." Carina shut the door to the cabinet and locked it. She could tell I wasn't going to listen. "Just don't touch your face. Remember what I said about that stuff. It doesn't take much to kill you."

I looked around outside and examined some of the surrounding structures. I didn't want any of this near the animals, so I had to be selective. I looked at a couple more sheds before I found the right place.

Perfect, I thought.

I found a shovel and entered the pump house. It wasn't much of a structure. It was just a small shed with metal siding located at the back of the property. It housed the well pump, a common feature of homes located outside city limits. There was no floor, just gravel. Pipes just barely visible aboveground plunged deep into the water table. The pump on top brought the water to the surface and provided Carina's place with fresh water. I placed the drugs aside and used the shovel to pull back some of the gravel. Once dirt was visible, I dug a shallow hole, then centered the two packages at the bottom of it. I put the dirt back and evenly placed the gravel on top.

It looks like I was never even here, I thought. *No one will ever suspect it.*

I shut the door to the pump house and returned the shovel to where I'd found it. Then I went back to the lab. Carina was standing right at the door when I entered.

"Colt, why are you using my place for this?"

"It's all I could do on short notice."

"Colt ..."

"I'm calling Will now."

I took out my phone and tapped in his number. I looked at Carina while I listened to the ringtone. Carina watched me. She was anxious to see what Will said.

"Colt?" said Will. "You said we were even. I can't do any more favors."

"Relax, Will. I'm not calling for a favor." I paused for a second as Carina and I stared at one another. "You're not going to believe this."

"With you involved, I probably will."

I explained all the events in detail. Carina teared up as I recounted the ones concerning Tempest. She looked down for a little bit. I could tell she was still very upset over the mare.

"Colt," Will began, "for someone who lives in a small rural town, you manage to attract some of the craziest people on the planet."

"I know. Just my luck, I guess. What do I do now?"

There was a pause.

"Here's what I want you to do. Try to call Chambon and Mrs. Philippe. Explain to them that you have their horse. If you don't call, it might look suspicious. Explain that you took the horse to the vet to be checked out. You were concerned … No, don't say that." He paused again. "We want them to come to us so we can talk to them. I don't want them to be suspicious. Just tell them that you have their horse and that it's ready to be picked up."

"I can do that. I'll try reaching out as soon as we hang up."

"I'm heading to Carina's now. I'm going to notify my boss. We'll be there in a little bit."

"I'll tell Carina the cavalry is on the way." I looked at Carina, and she let out a sigh of relief. Will and I said our goodbyes and hung up.

"Thank God," Carina said.

I sat down in a chair and called Chambon. I was just going to play it casual, like Will had recommended. I waited a few minutes for an answer, but there was nothing. I waited a couple more minutes and tried again. Still no answer. Then I tried Mrs. Philippe, with the same result. I ended the call and tapped my phone on my right leg, deep in thought. I looked up at Carina.

"I'm not sure I like this," I said. "You think someone got to them?"

Carina didn't say anything. She looked worried. I stood up, walked over to her, and gave her a hug.

"I'm going to run down to my office really quick," I said.

"Please don't leave," she replied.

"I just want to get the files I left on my desk. Will may need them."

"Colt, please don't ..."

"Everything will be fine. He will be here soon." I gave her another hug. "I'll leave Duke here to keep an eye on you. He's very good at guarding the home."

Carina reluctantly nodded her head in agreement.

"I'll be right back. I'm not going to let anything happen to you, promise."

~ 9 ~

"THE MAN DESERVES AN ACADEMY AWARD."

As the morning shifted into afternoon, the skies revealed a beautiful day. Bright white clouds reflected across the black hood of my truck. But the weather would soon change. Summertime thunderstorms were building in the far distance. The sounds of rumbling could already be heard.

As I drove across town, all kinds of questions and thoughts raced through my mind. *What have I walked into? Why won't Chambon and Mrs. Philippe answer? Are they aware that Tempest was being used as a mule to move drugs? Could Chambon be a drug runner? I can't believe I brought that horse to Carina's place. I basically dumped all of this into her lap. Will she ever forgive me?*

When my office came into view, I decided to change things up. I circled around the back like normal and slowly drove by to see if anything was out of place. Once I'd assured myself that everything looked normal, I drove my truck across the street and into the city hall parking lot. Since it was Saturday, everything was closed up. That made it easier for me to maneuver my truck around the curbs. I stopped once I was directly across the street from my place and put the truck in park. I pulled out my binoculars from the glove box for a closer look. I tried to look into the windows as best I could, but I didn't see much. My office stood silent.

I put the truck in drive, tapped the pedal, and the engine whistled as I circled out of the parking lot and behind city hall. Then I drove next door and parked my truck out of sight near the post office. I exited the cab and began taking a roundabout route toward the park.

I headed north for a couple blocks; then I turned east and walked an additional block, heading to the opposite end of the park. The traffic on main street sounded like it was getting busier. All the better. Maybe it would be a distraction for anyone inside my office. At this point, I would use anything for cover. The traffic, the trees, the monuments, anything available in the park. I wanted to get a better look at my office now that my truck was out of sight. If anyone was inside, they might feel comfortable and unintentionally show themselves in the windows.

I headed closer to my office and used a public restroom building as cover. I veered around the corner of the structure, pulled my binoculars out, and tried to look into the office windows. Everything still sat quietly. No movement of any kind.

"What are you lookin' at?"

I glanced behind me. It was Keke. Keke, as everyone called him, was homeless and had become a fixture of the town. He was often trying to help people with their bags in the grocery store parking lot or picking up cans—anything to earn an extra dollar or get something for free. I never could figure him out. Sometimes I talked with him, and he seemed completely normal. Other times, I saw him walking down the street swinging his shirt above his head and waving at cars as they passed. Either way, he seemed to enjoy his lifestyle. He never complained about it.

"What?" I asked. He'd caught me off guard. It took me a second to realize it was him.

"What are you lookin' at, Mr. Callacy?"

I went back to peering through my binoculars. "Keke, just call me Colt. We've talked about that before."

"What are you doing? Are you working on a case?"

"I just want to make sure everything is clear at my office."

"Are they bad guys?" Keke seemed excited at the thought of something new happening in town.

"Keke, don't run around town telling everyone that. I don't want anyone involved."

"These *are* bad guys! I didn't think things like that happened here. What did they do?"

"I'm not sure what's going on yet," I said. I looked back at Keke. "I reckon a lot of bad people are involved though. So don't let this get around."

"Let me see. I want to see."

I stopped Keke when he reached for my binoculars. "Keke, I don't want to you involved."

"I want to help."

"Keke, I don't have any money. My other clients won't even pay me. I don't even know how I'm going to make rent in a couple months."

"Come on, I don't want any money. I just want to help. This place is boring. There's finally some excitement, and I want to be a part of it."

"Why?"

"Because I want to tell people my story."

"What are you talking about?" I turned and gave him a puzzled look.

"I want to tell people how I assisted in solving a major crime."

"Who do you want to tell?"

"Anyone. Reporters, writers, anybody I can find. People pay a lot of money for exciting stories like this."

There was no getting rid of him.

"Alright, Keke, I tell you what. You want to help me? Hurry across the street and casually walk by my office so you can take a look inside. Then walk to the corner. If everything looks fine, wave your hand once, like this." I waved a hand to give him an example. "If something looks out of place, wave both of your hands, like this." I moved both arms for the second example. "Then you get the hell out of there and don't look back. Can you do that?"

"Yes, I can do that," Keke said as he nodded his head up and down.

"Hurry up then."

Keke started toward the street, then stopped and turned to me.

"What's wrong?" I asked.

"Do you have a cigarette?"

"What?"

"A cig." He started moving his arms around like a director describing a scene to his actors. All out in the open, of course, where everyone could see him. "It might make things look more casual and real if I walk by smoking a cig. I could casually window-shop while I smoke."

"Window shop where? At the barber, the well company? What are you talking about?" I shook my head in disbelief.

"Think about it. It's like an image from *The Saturday Evening Post.*"

"Would you just go and look!" I said. "I don't even smoke."

"I thought all cowboys smoke."

"This one doesn't!"

Keke turned back and hurried across the street when there was a break in traffic. When he got to the sidewalk on the other side, he clasped his hands behind his back and started whistling. He started looking into some of the windows as he made his way past the old storefronts. He even lifted his old fedora as a woman walked by him. She smiled at the gesture.

So much for being inconspicuous, I thought.

Once Keke was in front of my office, he slowed down and carefully looked in the windows as he walked by. Then he put his head down and grabbed the brim of his hat like he was trying to cover his face. He picked up the pace and hurried to the corner.

He looked like he had an answer for me and wanted to deliver it quickly.

Keke turned and looked back at me. I anxiously waited for his signal. He waved once. I tipped my hat with two fingers as a signal that I'd received his message. Keke then turned and hurried across the street before disappearing around the corner.

The man deserves an Academy Award, I said to myself.

~ 10 ~

"I HAVE FAITH IN YOU."

A storm continued to build in the distance, mushroom-like clouds rising high in the sky. The rolling sounds of thunder became more frequent. The sun was still bright and welcoming, but that wouldn't last for long.

After I received the okay from Keke, I hurried across the street once there was a break in traffic. I pulled my key out as I walked toward the front door of my office. If there was someone inside and they knew my routine, I might catch them off guard. They would probably be waiting for me to enter from around back.

I glanced in the windows quickly as I approached the old storefront. Everything looked okay. I unlocked the old wooden door, gave it a hard push, and entered. Then I shut the door behind me, giving it another good push until I heard the lock engage. The sunlight started to disappear thanks to the approaching storm, darkening the room some. Upon first glance, everything seemed fine. It wasn't until I noticed my desk that I realized my worries had come true. The files I had left earlier were gone.

My feet froze in place as reality set in, and I realized I might have walked into a dangerous situation. I paused to see if I could hear anybody inside. The silence was only disturbed by the soft sound of thunder from afar and the ticks of the pendulum clock echoing off the walls of the old building. I was still curious. Maybe it was in my nature. I leaned forward just to look around the corner down the dark hall. I didn't see any movement except for the dim natural light reflecting off the pendulum of the clock down the hall. I reached into my back pocket and pulled out my phone. I looked down at the screen and began searching for Will's number.

"Don't even think about it."

I looked up and saw the outline of a dark figure emerge from the bedroom. As it came closer, the dim light from the windows revealed the figure to be Chambon. He was holding a pistol. Chambon said something in Spanish. Behind him, two more figures appeared, both carrying machine guns of some type.

"Lock the phone and hand it to me," Chambon said. His sophisticated New Orleans accent was gone. It still sounded like it was from New Orleans but was much rougher than before. He was becoming impatient. He held the pistol in his right hand and stretched his left hand out, waiting for me to give him the phone. He waved the fingers on his left hand and raised his eyebrows. "Phone, please. You're trying my patience."

I handed Chambon my phone. He checked the screen to make sure my call had not gone through. Then he turned it off and handed it to one of the accompanying gunmen. Chambon said something to him in Spanish. The gunman took the phone, placed it on the table in the hall, and began destroying it with the butt of his gun. The other gunman strapped his gun on his shoulder, hurried to the front windows, and shut all the blinds. Then Chambon turned on a light.

"Mr. Callacy," he began. "I'm sorry—Colt, as you like to be called. I'm not too familiar with this town. But if it's like any other place in small-town USA, I'm willing to bet there are many sets of eyes watching us right now. That is something I cannot risk."

Chambon turned and talked to the man who had just finished destroying my phone. The man disappeared into my kitchen and reappeared with two jackets. They weren't mine. The gunmen proceeded to wrap their guns in the jackets. Chambon put his pistol into a holster he had strapped around his chest under his suit jacket.

"We're going to take a ride," Chambon said. "We're going to step out the back door and walk to our car. If anyone asks, you are going to tell them that we are clients. Understand?"

"I do," I responded. I was still frozen in place. I guess realization was still setting in. I had worked many cases in the past, most of them small. None of them could have prepared me for this.

"Relax," Chambon continued. "If I wanted you dead, you would be dead now." He reached into his jacket, pulled out a silencer pinched between his thumb and index finger, and waved it near my face. "Believe me, no one would even hear it." He put the silencer back into his pocket.

"What do you want me to tell them in case they do ask?" I asked. "Sometimes these people try to find out what I'm working on. Not to mention, you guys stick out like a sore thumb." I looked Chambon up and down. "I can't remember the last time I saw someone wearing a suit like yours walking down the sidewalk. Like you said, it's a small town. Some people can be inquisitive."

"You tell them we are clients, and then we all walk away." Chambon was aggravated with my response. "Don't get on my nerves."

The gunmen flanked me, and Chambon led the way as we went down the hall and out the back door. The sun was long gone, and the thunder was getting closer. We walked about a block into the neighborhood behind my place before we came upon a black SUV with tinted windows. It was hard to see inside.

"Get in the back," Chambon said.

I stepped up into the vehicle and sat down on the bench. One gunman sat next to me, Chambon took the front passenger seat, and the other gunman drove. As we pulled out, Chambon said something to the gunman next to me, who reached into his pocket and pulled out a pair of handcuffs. He motioned for me to hold my arms out. I was reluctant at first.

"Put your arms out," said Chambon. "Lean forward in the chair first."

I complied and the gunman put my arms behind my back and handcuffed me. Then he pushed my chest slightly, signaling for me to lean back. I reluctantly complied again. He pulled out a handkerchief, removed my hat, and blindfolded me.

"If you know what's best for you," began Chambon, "you'll just sit back and be quiet. It's going to be a little bit until we reach our destination." He then started talking in Spanish to the other gunmen.

All I could do was sit, listen, and think. I could hear heavy raindrops start to hit the SUV. They were loud and slow at first, signaling a heavy downpour was soon to come. The driver handled the car roughly. He hit the brakes quickly, and he seemed to swerve a lot. I wondered if he even had a license. Every time he hit the brakes and jerked us around, Chambon would say something in Spanish, and they would all laugh.

About an hour passed before the SUV slowed down to a crawl and turned onto a gravel road. The gravel crunched under the weight of the wheels as we slowly rolled along, only disturbed by the occasional rock flying from under the tires and hitting the undercarriage of the vehicle. After about five minutes, the car stopped. The driver said something, and Chambon replied back to him. Then I heard a loud screech that sounded like an old garage door opening. When the screeching stopped, the driver hit the gas, causing us to jerk back. Then he hit the brake. The man next to me said something, and they all laughed again.

I felt two bumps before the SUV began traveling on a smooth surface. The vehicle came to another stop. I heard the screeching sound behind us before everyone began to exit the cab. The door beside me opened, and I felt someone grab my right arm and pull me out. I carefully felt around with my feet to keep my balance. My captor was at least patient.

"Alright, Colt, right this way." It was Chambon leading me.

The afternoon heat and humidity hit me hard as I stepped out of the vehicle. It was raining hard, too. From the sound of it, the structure had a metal roof; the heavy afternoon rain echoed throughout the building.

"Come here, Colt," Chambon said in a friendly manner. He continued to lead me by the arm. "Now lean back." I did as he requested and found a chair under me. Then I felt another set of hands strapping my torso and legs to the chair. Chambon let go of my arm and a set of fingers quickly danced around on the back of my head before the blindfold was removed.

My eyes were not ready for the sudden burst of light. I quickly closed my eyes and pulled my head to the right. After a few seconds, I shook my head and carefully looked around. Chambon was standing there with the blindfold in his hand, and the two gunmen were standing behind him with their weapons in hand, doing their best to look intimidating. It looked like we were in an old garage of some sort. The floor was cement, with old oil spills scattered around. The metal roof and walls were rusty and dinged in a few places, showing the scars of a rough life.

"I'm just going to jump to the chase," Chambon said. "Where are the drugs?"

"I don't know what you are talking about, Chambon," I replied. "I just found the mare. I was getting ready to call you in fact."

Chambon laughed and walked over to a black Lincoln Continental parked on the other side of the garage, pulled out an axe handle from the trunk, and walked back to me.

"Colt, don't play this game with me. This isn't TV. This is real."

Chambon swung the axe handle and hit the front portion of my lower right leg. I let out a yell of agonizing pain. I naturally tried to lean forward, but I was strapped tight to the chair.

"Hurts, doesn't it?" Chambon placed one end of the axe handle down on the floor like a cane and leaned on it. "Now, where are the drugs?"

I didn't say anything. I was still recovering from the shock of the blow, which trembled throughout my nervous system.

"I've been monitoring your movements," Chambon continued. "Are the drugs still with that vet?" I didn't say anything. "Colt, you're making this harder than it has to be." He picked up the handle and hit my leg again, and I let out a deep holler.

"Damn it, Chambon!" I paused for a minute and lifted my head up. "She doesn't have anything to do with this."

"Then you better start talking." Chambon paused and smiled. He leaned down and looked at me as he started talking in a smooth and collected manner. "She's a cute girl. It would be a shame if something were to happen to her."

I didn't say anything. The smile disappeared from Chambon's face as he grew impatient. "Okay," he said.

He stood up and placed the end of the axe handle against my leg where he'd hit it repeatedly. Then he began twisting the handle. I starting moaning and yelling. Chambon began biting his tongue and smiling as he worked at sending wave after wave of pain throughout my body.

"I called the police and turned everything over to them. We don't have your drugs!"

Chambon stopped and put the axe handle down. The gunmen looked at him. The smile quickly disappeared from his face.

"Well, that's bad luck for you, Colt. Bad luck for you and bad luck for me if that's true." He looked me up and down. "I have a hard time imagining a country hick like you letting go of that kind of money."

"You think I still have the shipment ..."

Chambon's phone rang, and he answered it. He put the axe handle over his shoulder using his other hand. He slowly walked away from the group as he talked. I could only make out part of the conversation.

"How's everything over there?" he asked. He paced slowly as he talked. "Good," he said. "Very good." He listened to the other end of the line before continuing. "He doesn't know a thing. You've got nothing to worry about. Just follow my lead and you'll be fine. Once we wrap things up here, we'll disappear."

Chambon ended the call and started walking back toward me.

"You're in luck, Colt. The gods are with you. There might be some hope for you and that vet."

I looked up at him.

"I thought I was going to have to make a mess of you just to get you to talk, but we have something much easier to work with now. We have that cute little vet of yours. We snagged her right before the police arrived."

What have I done? I thought to myself. I closed my eyes as realization overwhelmed me. *I should have listened to Carina.*

"Hey," Chambon said. He tapped the bottom of my chin with his finger. I opened my eyes, and he smiled.

"I swear, Chambon," I began, "if you harm Carina, I'll break every bone in your body. I don't know how or when, but I will do it."

Chambon looked back at the guards. "We found his weak spot." The guards just looked at him. He shook his head and repeated it in Spanish. The guards smiled at the good news before Chambon turned his attention back to me. "She'll be fine as long as you get my shipment."

Chambon said something else in Spanish, and the guards strapped on their guns, walked over, and untied me. Then Chambon returned to the dark Lincoln, reached into a bag in the back seat, and pulled out a phone.

"Take this," he said. "I don't know how you're going to do it. But I need those drugs. I'm going to give you a call at nine tonight. Have everything together by then. At ten, we'll make the exchange.

"Chambon," I said, "the police have the drugs. How will I get those back?"

"If you want her back, you'll find a way. I have faith in you."

Chambon took the blindfold and slipped it back over my eyes. I caught his face break into another smile as he disappeared out of sight.

~ 11 ~

"WE'RE GOING TO HAVE A LONG
NIGHT AHEAD OF US."

The thunderstorm had dissipated into a light drizzle by the time the SUV made its way back to town. The vehicle slowed and turned into the parking lot of my place. We bounced around as the right tires hit a pothole, causing water to spray the undercarriage. The driver hit the brakes, causing everyone to slide forward before the vehicle came to a complete stop.

Chambon said something in Spanish, and the gunman next to me removed my blindfold. It took a couple seconds for my eyes to readjust to the light. I looked out the window and saw the rain running down the outside of the window come into focus. I turned my head, and Chambon peered at me from the passenger seat.

"Remember," he began, "I will call you at nine, and we will make the exchange at ten."

My guard leaned over me, unlocked the cuffs, and handed me my Stetson. Then he signaled for me to exit. I opened the door, grabbed the handle above my head, and pulled myself out of the vehicle. I took my time finding my footing. My right leg was killing me. Once I was out, the guard shut the door, and the dark vehicle exited the parking lot and disappeared out of sight. I looked around the parking lot. It looked like the heavy rain had already passed. The thunder still roared across the sky in the distance. The air was much cooler now, and everything was soaked. There was a

~ 71 ~

slight mist, as well as the sounds of heavy drops dripping from the nearby trees and shrubs.

I fell forward and caught myself with my hands as I tried to walk toward my back door. My right leg was in bad shape. It was hard for me to put pressure on it without sending a shock of pain throughout my body. I took a second to catch my breath, then slowly got to my feet.

"Colt!"

I looked behind me. It was Keke. He came running up to me. He'd been using my neighbor's lean-to to stay out of the rain.

"Colt! Are you okay?"

"I'm fine, Keke."

"Let me help you."

Keke grabbed my right arm and began helping me inside my place. It took me a bit to reach the door as I limped along. When we entered, we both paused. Every room in my place had been turned inside out. Every drawer had been pulled out and dumped on the floor. The contents of the closets had been tossed around and thrown across the floor. Even the door of the toolshed had been pried open. Every room was hit.

"Your safe looks okay," said Keke.

I took a look for myself. It appeared untouched.

"I see that," I said. "I guess they didn't have any way to get inside ... or they didn't have time." I rubbed my forehead with the palm of my hand. "I've got to get to Carina's, fast. Can you help me to my truck? It's parked across the street."

"You got it, Colt."

Keke assisted me across the street. It took a few minutes given my slow pace. Keke also thought it would be best to use the crosswalk at the corner instead of attempting to hurry across the street in between fast-moving traffic. Once I was at my truck, Keke helped me into the cab, then looked down at my leg.

"Your leg is giving you a lot of trouble," he said. "Do you want me to drive?"

"Keke, do you even know how to drive?"

"I saw my dad do it many times." He paused before continuing. "I drove once when I was in the Army."

That stopped me in my tracks.

"You're a veteran?" I asked.

Keke shrugged his shoulders in agreement.

"What are you doing out in the streets?"

He shrugged his shoulders again. "Making a living."

I thought about his reply before I shook my head slightly and lifted my eyebrows in acknowledgment. "Take care of yourself, Keke."

"Watch your back." He smiled and gave me a thumbs-up. "I know we're going to get these guys!"

I gave him a two-finger salute with the brim of my hat as a sign of agreement before shutting the truck door. I fired up the truck, put it in reverse, and hit the accelerator. The Ford's V8 jerked me before I quickly slammed down on the brake. My leg was giving me a hard time. Keke ran up to my window, so I rolled it down.

"Are you sure you don't want me to drive?" he asked.

"I'm sure, Keke."

I put the truck in forward and lightly tapped the pedal. The truck slowly rolled forward as I applied pressure with my foot.

"Looking good," Keke said. He walked alongside the truck, acting like a spotter.

"I got it now," I said. "Thanks, Keke."

He gave me another thumbs-up. I rolled up the window and picked up speed. Keke stopped and watched me turn the corner until I was out of sight.

When I pulled up to Carina's place, there were several police cars in the parking lot in front of the clinic. I recognized Will's police truck right off the bat. I pulled into the parking lot and took up a couple spaces instead of trying to maneuver my truck into one. Once the truck was parked, I struggled out of the cab.

Will heard the diesel and came walking out. He was a built person and could look intimidating at times. On the job, he walked around with his chest out, always ready to face the next challenge. Deep inside that tough guy persona, though, was a fun person who got along with everyone and had a sense of humor to ease the pressures of life. When he first joined the force, his new partners joked about his size and began referring to him as "Mr. Clean" because his arms and upper torso seemed like they were roughly the same size as those of the man used for the company logo. He wasn't always that big, from what I remember. He was skinny in the National Guard, like me, but he just kept working out as he went into the force. He was a dedicated person.

"Colt," Will began, "what the hell is going on?" I struggled around the front of the truck. "Why are you limping?" he continued.

"Has anyone seen Carina?" I asked.

"I was the first one here. I couldn't find anyone. I found Duke. He's been beat up."

"Oh, no," I said. I started to make my way inside, but he grabbed my arm and stopped me. "Carina's assistant is looking him over now. She says he'll be fine, nothing they can't fix."

My mind was racing. My thoughts jumped back to Carina. I started to head inside like I was going to look for her.

"Colt!" Will stopped me again. "Pull yourself together!"

I stopped trying to push myself inside. "Are you sure she's not here?" I asked.

"Colt, we've checked every square inch of this place. She's not here. Her house and office have been turned inside out. What's going on? Where have you been?" Will looked down at my leg. "Why are you limping?"

"Chambon has got her."

"Who?"

"Chambon ... he's got her. He kidnapped her."

"What?" I stumbled on my leg again and Will grabbed my right arm. "Let's head inside and you can tell me what's going on."

Will helped me into the office and sat me down in one of the chairs located in the front lobby. Carina's assistant was there. She was in her early twenties and working toward her degree at university. I didn't know her well. I'd only met her a couple times.

"How's Duke?" I asked.

"He'll be fine," she said. "He had a couple bones that needed to be reset. Duke will make a full recovery, though. I gave him some meds to ease the pain. He's probably going to sleep for a while. He needs his rest."

"Thank you," I said.

She looked down at my leg. "Let me take a look at that. I've treated a couple cowboys when we've done ranch calls."

"You've treated a couple cowboys?" I asked with a puzzled look.

"A couple times," she said. "Carina treats most of them, though. After we finish with the livestock. We're all animals, you know."

"My God," Will said. "I'm going to pretend I didn't hear that." He waved his arms back and forth, hoping not to hear anything else. "I should turn you all in."

I lifted my right pant leg, pulled off my boot, and lowered my sock so she could take a look.

"Damn, Colt," said Will. "What the hell?"

My leg was swollen, and there was a large, dark bruise where Chambon had hit it repeatedly.

"Ouch!" the vet said. She examined it up close. "May I feel it?"

"Whatever you think is best," I replied.

She began running her fingers over the bruise. I grit my teeth each time she applied pressure to a certain area.

"Looks like it's a bruised bone," she said. "It doesn't seem broken. Just keep an eye on it. It's going to take weeks to heal. It's going to hurt like hell, too."

"Now, what happened?" asked Will.

"That was Chambon. He hit me with an axe handle."

"What?" he said.

Carina's assistant was curious too. She looked up at me. A couple deputies entered the room at this point.

"After I finished talking with you, I left. I headed to my office to pick up a couple files from my case. I thought they might help you. My plan was to grab them and return here before you arrived. I shouldn't have left ..."

"Colt," Will began, "just tell us what happened."

"When I got back to the office, Chambon and a couple guys were waiting for me. They blindfolded me and took me to some secluded garage. He wanted his drugs."

"Did you recognize any of the guys with him?" Will asked. "Or did they say anything?"

"No," I said. "They didn't speak English. Chambon talked to them both in Spanish. Each one had a machine gun of some sort."

"When did they tear up your leg?" asked one of the deputies.

"Chambon's intention was to beat the information out of me, but someone called him and told him they had picked up Carina. That's when he made a deal with me instead."

"What was the deal?" asked Will.

"He gave me this phone." I pulled the phone out of my pocket and showed Will. He began examining it.

"It's a burner phone," he said.

"Chambon said he's going to call me at nine and tell me where to meet him at ten. He said we'll do an exchange. They'll hand over Carina if I hand over the drugs."

"Does he know we're involved?" Will asked.

"I told Chambon that. He didn't seem to care. He said he just wanted his shipment."

"If he's taking a risk like that," Will began, "he's in a tight spot. He's feeling the pressure on his end from somewhere."

"That's what I was thinking," I said. "A boss or somebody."

"Where are the drugs now?" asked Will.

They should be in the drug cabinet. I led the team into Carina's lab. Carina's assistant grabbed the key and opened the door. I pulled both bags out and showed Will. "Carina verified it as carfentanil."

"She was certain?" asked one of the deputies.

"Carina's good," said Will. "I guarantee this is carfentanil if she says it is." He picked up one of the bags. "There's a fortune here in these two bags alone. This was all of it?"

I hesitated. I hated to lie to a close friend. But I just had a hunch.

"Yes, that's all we found. She also said to be careful with it. It's very potent."

"I've heard of this stuff," Will said. "But I've never dealt with it." He looked at me. "I don't even think we tracked this stuff in the National Guard. It's rare you hear about this drug. I can't believe it's here in Levy County."

"What do you think?" I asked.

Will put the bags down and looked at his watch. Then he thought for a minute before slightly nodding his head like he was agreeing with a thought he had. "Okay, we've got a few hours to prep ... and we're going to have a long night ahead of us. But we're going to do it. Let's bring Carina home."

~ 12 ~

"JUST RIDE IN LIKE A COWBOY."

Clear skies revealed the sun beginning to set over the farms outside Williston. The afternoon storm had delivered its rain for the day, leaving everything soaked for the night. The morning sun would dry everything the next day, repeating the daily summertime cycle. The officers and I had made our way to the county seat of Bronson. A small town compared to Williston, Bronson was much older, with a long history, and was once a major destination along the Florida Railroad. Now, the rails were long gone, and the town was in much the same shape as Williston. Regardless, it had that small-town feel that many cherished.

We were all bunched into a tight room, circling around a large table. Will's boss was standing in front of everyone, reviewing the plan for tonight. Sheriff Thomas "Tom" Harding was a name I had come to know well. He was a towering figure, with broad shoulders and a medium build. His shaved head and stern look gave more of the impression of a drill sergeant than a sheriff. He had a rough, down-to-business attitude most of the time. He'd basically hated me ever since one of my cases had crossed paths with one of his.

We reviewed the plan several times like a well-choreographed war strategy. Sheriff Harding would stop, point at one of us randomly, and ask that person questions about the plan in his deep voice. If he called on you, it was intimidating. There was a method to his madness. He wanted to ensure that everyone knew their part of the plan without hesitation, no questions asked.

"Colt." He pointed at me and asked, "When Chambon calls, what are you going to do?"

"I'm going to get the location of the handoff and take note of anything I hear in the background that may help you guys identify his current location."

"What might you be listening for?"

"Anything," I said. "Someone talking in the background, a radio, a siren, anything."

"We've identified the locations of many fugitives that way. What may seem unimportant may be very vital to us. On the other hand, Chambon could be prepared for that."

"Can't we track these calls?" asked a deputy.

"Normally, we could," replied Sheriff Harding. "But we just don't have the time. They're not giving us much of a window to work with. Colt, once we have the location, what's next?"

"I'm going to take my truck to the address with both bags. Just like Chambon asked. Keep it casual. We want Chambon to feel comfortable and not suspect a thing."

He pointed to Will. "What about you, Will?"

"I'm going to follow behind at a distance in an unmarked truck and keep an eye on Colt while reporting what I see to you guys. My main job is to alert the team if Chambon tries to change plans."

"What about you?" Harding looked at one of his deputies. I'd met him once. He was from Jacksonville and was more of a tech guy.

"I'm going to track Colt's truck and report to you guys in case Will gets separated. Colt's truck is ready to go. I've placed the tracker on it, and I will know the location of his truck each step of the way."

The thought of having a tracker on my truck annoyed me. I just didn't like it. They hadn't asked my permission. You just don't mess with another man's truck. It's not right.

"I've also placed another tracker in the duffel bag carrying the drugs," continued the deputy. "Chambon may be expecting that though."

"What about Colt?" asked Sheriff Harding.

"He refuses to wear any devices," replied the deputy.

"Colt ..." began the sheriff.

"I'm not wearing a tracker, nor am I wearing a microphone," I said.

Will jumped in. "Colt ..."

The others in the room looked at each other. I could tell some were afraid to spar with their boss.

"I'm not doing it," I said.

"Not going to do it, huh?" the sheriff growled. "I imagine you're going to just ride in like a cowboy and save the day, right?"

"With all due respect, sheriff," I said, "Chambon's guards are from South America, each armed with a machine gun. For all I know, they were probably born with guns in their hands. Probably grew up during some revolution. I don't want to get on their bad side."

"Colt," Will insisted. "You'll be fine. We will know your location the entire time. We've got your back."

"Unless Chambon is prepared for that," I said. "If they find a wire on me, they may kill me on sight. Carina, too. Honestly, I'm not too keen on having that tracker on my truck or that duffel bag."

"Those trackers stay," demanded Sheriff Harding. You could have heard a pen drop. He was famous for his temper and stern ways, and many on his crew learned that quickly. I could tell he was already annoyed with me. Despite that, he knew time was running out and decided to continue going over his plan. "Will is going to be our eyes and report to me. We'll follow from afar. I'll make the final decision when to move in on these guys." He paused. "Are there any questions?"

"Is the DEA going to be involved?" asked Will. "Are they going to offer any help?"

"I've notified them" the sheriff replied. "They are involved, but it's such short notice that we're basically on our own."

"Has anyone tried to reach out to Mrs. Philippe?" I asked. "To warn her about Chambon."

"We contacted the Ocala police," began Will. "They sent an officer to check on her, but she had checked out. According to the front desk, she went back to France."

"Are there any other questions?" Sheriff Harding looked around the room, but everyone was silent. "A friend of mine is helping us tonight. He lent us the use of his helicopter. I deputized him so he can work with us. He'll be acting as pilot, and I will be his passenger. I just want to be able to move fast." A thought struck him. "That reminds me. I need to deputize you, Colt, as much as I hate to. It's the only way you can transport those drugs legally. Is a badge going to bother you, too? Or do you want to act like a vigilante tonight? Old West style?"

The room was silent again.

"Whatever you have to do," I replied.

"At least we finally agree on something," he said. He paused for a few seconds. "I don't know what it is about PIs. I just don't like them. I always think they like to work outside the law."

I didn't respond. The room was still silent.

"We should be prepared for anything Chambon throws our way," Sheriff Harding said as he scanned his audience, alleviating some of the tension. "Remember, I'll give the final signal to move in."

Suddenly, the sheriff was interrupted mid-speech. The moment we'd all been anticipating had arrived: The burner phone began ringing in front of us all.

"This is it," replied Sheriff Harding.

~ 13 ~

"WHEN THEY GET EVERYTHING THEY WANT..."

Everyone was quiet as the burner phone rang and vibrated across the table. Not a soul moved as we watched it intently. The moment we had been waiting for had arrived. Tension could be felt among the entire crew. All the anticipation, the prepping, and the worrying boiled down to this moment. No one could foresee how the operation would play out, but the time had come.

I felt my stomach drop as the phone rang. I had not anticipated that. I'd thought I would be ready for it, but I was still worried. I reached down to pick up the phone, but Sheriff Harding grabbed my hand.

"Remember," he said. "Listen for anything in the background. Anything minor could be very vital to us." I nodded my head in agreement. I still felt a little dazed as the situation continued to unfold. "Try to keep them on the phone for as long as possible."

I nodded my head again, and he let go. I picked up the phone and answered it on the next ring.

"Hello?" I wasn't sure how this conversation would go.

"Colt?" said Chambon. I listened to the background. It was quiet except for the echo from his voice. "There's an old garage south of Williston. From the looks of things, it's been abandoned for some time. There's nothing out here but dirt roads." He gave the location. "Do you know where I'm talking about?"

"I do," I replied. "I think it's an old machine shop."

"Good," he said. "Meet us here at ten o'clock. I'll be watching for your truck. If you have a tail, Carina's dead."

"Wait, Chambon—" It was no use. He hung up the phone immediately, and I looked up. "He didn't want to stay on the phone."

"He's worried about being tracked," Sheriff Harding said. "What did he say?"

"He said to meet him at that old machine shop south of Williston. I think they used to fix equipment for the peanut farms."

"Did you hear anything else?" asked Will.

"No, just an echo. He's got to be at the garage."

"Did he say anything about Carina?" Will continued.

"Meet him at ten. He'll be looking for my truck. If I have a tail, she dies."

"That's original," said Sheriff Harding. He looked at everyone around the table. "Let's go."

Sheriff Harding quickly swore me in as a deputy, and the tech deputy handed me a brown duffel bag containing the drugs. We then exited the room and went to our stations, putting the battle plan into motion. As Will and I left the building, the humid night hit us both like a wall. There was not a breeze to be found. It was unusual. The moon was just about full and the night was clear, yet the crickets and cicadas lay silent. It was as if they knew something in the world wasn't right. I rubbed my neck with my right hand as I carried the bag with my left. I was drenched in sweat.

"What a miserable night," I said as I limped along. "I should've never taken that horse to Carina's."

"Hey," Will said. "Don't be like that. That doesn't help Carina. We'll get her back."

"I should have taken that horse directly to the park."

"Colt, you didn't know. Don't be hard on yourself."

I was quiet for a minute.

"Will, are you sure you can stay out of sight?" I asked. "I'll never forgive myself if something happens to her. They were adamant that I be alone."

"They won't even know I'm present, Colt." Will could tell I was still worried. "Besides, these guys usually don't want anything to do with a hostage. It's too messy and draws a lot of attention. They don't want any of that. They would rather get rid of the hostage and take the shipment. When they get everything they want, they'll give her up."

I opened the cab of my truck and started to climb into the driver's seat.

"You okay?" he asked. He could see my leg was giving me trouble.

"I'm alright," I replied. I situated myself in the seat and placed the bag in the passenger seat. "I'll get it looked at closer when this thing is all over with."

As I pulled out of the parking lot, Will gave me a thumbs-up from inside an unmarked police car. He pulled out behind me. As I exited the lot and drove onto the highway, I looked in my rearview mirror just to make sure Will was staying out of sight. I saw the headlights of his car slowly fall back into the distance.

With the diesel humming along, I began recounting the conversation Will and I had just concluded. That last part struck me: *"When they get everything they want..."* I thought about the two bags buried in the pump house. I could stop at Carina's and get them, but Sheriff Harding might arrest me for holding out on them. That didn't bother me at this point. I was more concerned about Carina than anything else. But I was running out of time, too. The clock was ticking. I was going to have to negotiate with Chambon. I didn't have a choice. I'd just tell him the police had the other two. It could work. Especially if he wanted to move fast.

The location of the garage was very secluded. I had been there a couple times when Carina was showing me around the county, talking about growing up here. There were hardly any homes out here, just farms, and dirt roads stretched in all directions off the paved highway. It would be easy for anyone not familiar with the area to get lost.

As I pulled off the highway onto the next dirt road I came across, I turned on my high beams and looked around. The road ahead was rough and secluded. There was not a light or street sign to be found. It wasn't a road maintained by the county, for sure. I put the truck in four-wheel drive and rode the brakes as the vehicle rolled over deep ruts. After a couple of miles, I came to the first intersection. Whoever had last leveled the road had piled dirt along all sides of the junction. They must've been in a hurry ... or hadn't cared. I could see the road acted like a trough during downpours. There were ripples in the road from the pooling water. At this point, a cloud covered the light of the moon. I pulled out a flashlight from my glove box, rolled down the window, and shined the light on the lone street sign to find out the street name and get my location.

I had another mile to go before I turned. I turned the flashlight off and continued across the intersection. I could hear the sound of the diesel echoing in the darkness around me. The road did not improve. It continued to deteriorate as I traveled deeper into the woods of pines and palmettos. I wondered how Will could possibly keep up with me.

When I reached the next intersection, I stopped and checked the street sign. It was time to turn. I turned and continued to ride the brake. This time, the road was even worse. Someone had driven a tractor back here recently, and the tire treads had left a deep, rough impression on the road. I could feel the steering wheel shaking in my hands. Gravel pounded the bottoms of the wheel wells. I wanted to drive faster to get to Carina, but I didn't want to risk breaking down. I had no choice but to drive slowly. I only had a few more miles to go.

I continued to ride the brakes until I saw the reflection of another vehicle in my headlights. It was moving fast. I hit the brake quickly bringing the truck to an abrupt stop. The SUV from earlier drove out of a clearing in the woods and came to a sliding stop in front of me. The driver had left the lights off to conceal their movements. Both gunmen from earlier jumped out of the front seats and came running up to my truck with their guns pointed at me. They were yelling at me in Spanish. I had no idea what they were saying, but the guns said it all clearly: *Comply.*

I put the truck in park as they approached and put both my hands up so they could see them. They continued to shout. They looked worried. One reached over and opened the door. I kept my hands up and carefully stepped out. Once my left foot was on the ground, one of the gunmen—my captor from earlier—grabbed my left arm, pulled me from the cab, and pushed me flat to the ground. He then grabbed both my hands and put them in cuffs behind my back. I looked over at the cab. The other gunman scanned it quickly, saw the duffel bag, and grabbed it. Then they picked me up by the cuffs and hurried back to the SUV. My leg had not improved much from earlier, so I was more or less dragged along. My captor strapped his gun to his shoulder, swung open the back door, and began shoving me inside. When I landed on my side, he pushed my legs over just enough to slam the door shut behind me.

At this point, the driver was already behind the wheel, and he yelled something to the other gunman, who jumped into the passenger seat. The driver turned on the lights and floored it. I didn't think the vehicle was designed to take this much of a pounding. The rough terrain caused everything inside the cab to rattle violently, and it felt like I sprang completely off the seat a couple times. While all this went on, the driver and passenger were shouting at one another. They feared something. They feared for their lives. It couldn't be just the police. These were people who had built a career running from the law; they knew the routine. The police wouldn't just kill them if they cooperated with their demands when captured.

The vehicle finally came to a halt as I heard the back wheels slide. The gunmen climbed out and slammed the doors shut. As I struggled to sit up in the seat, the door next to me swung open. My captor grabbed my shirt with both hands and pulled me out of the SUV. My right leg gave out when I put pressure on it, causing a jolt of pain throughout my body. I stumbled forward, but the gunman didn't care. He just dragged me along until I struggled back onto both my feet. I looked around to see where they had taken me.

It was a large clearing with a few trees around. The dirt road under my feet seemed to be packed tight. There were no homes or farms in sight. But that was the least of it. In front of me stood a small jet. The stairs were down, and Chambon was standing at the bottom of them. The windows were shut to conceal any lights from inside the cabin. Chambon began talking to the gunmen. He took the duffel bag from the driver and started looking through it.

"Was this all of it?" Chambon asked me. He'd caught me off guard. I hadn't been expecting that question. "Is this all of it?" he demanded again.

"Yes," I said. "The other bag ripped at some point. That's what killed Tempest."

Chambon examined the ripped bag, which was patched. "You didn't see anything else?" He had a stern look on his face, but he was also anxious. He wanted to move fast.

"Nothing," I said. "Carina didn't find anything else." It was a gamble, I knew. Carina could have been interrogated by Chambon. This could be a test to see whether our stories matched.

Chambon pulled the drugs out of the duffel bag and placed the packages on the stairs. He then walked away from the stairs and threw the duffel bag into the woods. He returned to the stairs and began examining each package. He ran his fingers around the clear wrapping and began applying pressure to certain spots. "Just making sure there's nothing else in here, like a tracker," he said.

"What about Carina?" I asked.

Chambon looked at me, then said something in Spanish. The gunmen grabbed my cuffs and dragged me up the stairs. Chambon followed. Once we were inside, one gunman put me in a seat, and the other pulled up the stairs and sealed the door shut. I heard the engines fire up as Chambon hurried to the cockpit. I looked around quickly for Carina, but I didn't see any sign of her. I leaned over in my seat and looked forward to see what was happening up front.

"Are we ready?" asked the pilot.

"We've got everything," Chambon replied. "Let's get out of here."

My captors sat down in the seats next to me, and I sat back when one lightly placed his arm against my chest and applied pressure. The other reached over and tightened my seat belt. Then they laid their guns in their laps and strapped themselves into their seats as well. I glanced at the guns for a moment. The thought of grabbing one and demanding Carina came to mind, but it was hopeless with my hands secured behind my back.

I heard the engines growl as we began to taxi along the dirt road.

"Chambon," the pilot said, "I need you to strap in. Sit down in that seat."

"Just go!" Chambon demanded.

"Chambon!"

I tried to look at the cockpit again without the gunmen noticing. I could just make the pilot and Chambon out. Chambon finally complied. He sat down in the seat next to the pilot and strapped in. He was panicking.

The jet started to pick up more speed. One of the men next to me clutched the arms of his seat. The other was a little more relaxed.

It seemed like we were just about to take off when a bright light flashed into the cockpit. Chambon put his hands in front of his face to block the light. The howl of the engines slowed down, and the plane began to lose speed. The gunmen next to me started to look around, curious as to what was happening outside the plane. Then I heard the popping sound of helicopter rotors.

"Stop the jet!" Sheriff Harding's menacing voice intensified over a loud bullhorn. "Stop the jet, now!"

"Hold on!" shouted the pilot. "We have one more shot at this!"

I could feel the jet turning around. Then the engines roared to life again.

"Come on," yelled Chambon. "Move it. Move it!"

"Shut up!" yelled the pilot.

Will's unmarked car finally entered the scene. It parked right in the path of the plane. The blue cation lights from the car glimmered throughout the cockpit. The jet finally came to a stop as the engines quieted down.

"Just go around!" yelled Chambon.

"Where?" said the pilot. "In the woods? I don't have enough room to turn around. Even if I could, there's a damn helicopter blocking the road behind us."

Chambon unstrapped his belt, jumped out of his seat, and came running back to the main cabin. He pulled his pistol out and ran up to me.

"Get up!" he demanded. He grabbed my shirt collar and started pulling me out of the seat. "Unstrap him, damn it!" He repeated himself in Spanish.

The man next to me unstrapped my seat belt, and Chambon pulled me out of my seat. He dragged me by my right arm toward the door. My leg slowed us down some.

"Hurry up damn you!" he yelled. He unsealed the door and lowered the stairs. The gunmen, meanwhile, undid their own seat belts and stepped toward the back of the cabin, out of sight.

By this time, the other deputies had arrived. Patrol cars of all sorts surrounded the plane. The officers were behind their vehicles, guns drawn. Chambon put his arm around my neck and put the pistol to my head. He hid the rest of his body behind mine.

"I want the road opened, now!" he yelled.

By this point, the pilot had come to the door, but he stayed just out of sight to avoid any possible gunfire.

"Chambon," began the pilot, "it's over. Put your hands up before they start shooting. Their bullets will pierce this plane like tinfoil. They'll kill us all." He looked over at the gunmen. "Put those guns down!" He pointed to the guns, then the floor. They understood what he meant and complied, but they continued to avoid the door.

Chambon turned and pointed the gun at the pilot. "Get back in your seat!"

I took my body weight and pushed Chambon against the door frame. He pushed back, kicked my leg, and put the gun back to my head.

"Don't do that again!" he said through his teeth. "I swear to God, I will blow your goddamn brains out for all to see, you damn hick."

At this point, Will started to approach. He still had his pistol drawn.

"Clear the road!" Chambon demanded. "Otherwise, I'll kill him."

"That dumb redneck doesn't mean anything to me," Will replied.

I turned my head slightly at the words.

"I promise I'll kill him!" Chambon repeated. He was tense.

"You'll just die next," Will responded calmly.

Chambon looked down and saw four red dots pointed at his exposed chest.

"Just put your gun down before this gets worse," Sheriff Harding interjected. He'd evidently exited the helicopter and joined the other deputies near the vehicles. He was becoming irritated.

"Just put it down!" demanded the pilot. "I'm not going to die for you. I just fly the plane."

Chambon was still refusing to comply. I decided to take action. I reached over with my cuffed hands, grabbed his belt, and leaned forward quickly, pulling him off his feet. We both lost our balance and rolled down the flight of stairs. Will and Sheriff Harding came running up, along with another deputy. When we landed at the bottom, everyone began yelling at once in mass confusion. Will and the deputy began fighting Chambon as they searched for his gun. Sheriff Harding continued to keep a gun trained on Chambon. The other deputies remained behind their cars, pointing their guns at the jet.

"I got it!" yelled the deputy. "I got the pistol right here!"

Will placed cuffs on Chambon and led him to a squad car. The deputy who'd assisted Will helped me to my feet and got me to safety behind one of the patrol trucks before helping Will with Chambon. Will reappeared shortly with the keys to my cuffs and unlocked them.

"Colt," said Sheriff Harding. He had moved to stand behind the vehicle next to us. "How many more are there?"

"The pilot and two others," I said. "The pilot is ready to give up. The others have put their guns down. The pilot speaks English, but the other two only speak Spanish."

"Pilot," yelled Harding. "Come out with your hands in the air!"

The pilot complied. He stepped out of the cabin and walked down the stairs. When he got to the bottom, he was directed to lift his shirt and spin around in place. Then he was told to turn around and walk backward toward the police. He obeyed the orders and was placed in cuffs and taken to a car.

Another deputy yelled in Spanish for one of the gunmen to come out. The officers repeated the process for him and then the other. As soon as the final gunman was put in cuffs, I darted up the flight of stairs quickly.

"Colt," yelled Will. "Wait!"

I didn't pay him any attention. I started scanning the interior of the cabin quickly. From the cockpit all the way to the rear. I checked the closets, bathrooms, everything.

"Carina!" I yelled. Nothing. Not one sound. "Carina! Where are you?"

Just silence. There was no one else on the plane. I limped toward the door. The officers were still pointing guns at the entrance. They lowered them when they saw me reappear. My arms were hanging at my sides. I put one hand up on the doorframe and leaned on it. I was overcome with a feeling of defeat.

Will looked at me. "Is she in there?"

~ 14 ~

"YOU MUST THINK CARINA IS A TRUMP CARD."

With night now completely draping the land, another world had completely awakened and taken over. The ordeal I'd just been through was a reminder of the other elements at play in this realm. In between the honest who were toughing out a hard living, there were others attempting to make an easy buck despite the cost, whatever that cost may be. But the line of squad cars that traveled back to Bronson, with criminals in custody, was a reminder that there was another force out there trying to keep crime at bay for everyone.

Will and Sheriff Harding brought Chambon into the station, holding him by his arms in case he decided to make a break for it. I limped behind all three men as we entered the station. Everyone in the sheriff's office was hard at work. One would never expect it from such a small county. The look on Chambon's face was one of beaten-down anger. Almost as if he were ready to give up.

"Colt," Will began, "go ahead and have a seat out here. We're going to book him. I'll get you in a minute."

I sat out in the lobby waiting for Will to return. As I sat there, I noted the other deputies bringing in Chambon's crew. The first gunman, the driver from earlier that day, was calm and kept to himself. He seemed to know the process well. He must've been through this situation before. I doubt he wanted to look at anyone or say anything for fear it may cause him more trouble in court.

The second gunman, the one who'd sat next to me in the back seat and restrained me, was a different case. He recognized me the moment the deputies opened the glass doors and led him into the lobby. He started yelling something in Spanish and began moving his arms back and forth like he wanted to break loose from the deputies. I just sat in my chair and watched. I reached into my pocket and slipped on a pair of brass knuckles I often kept with me just in case. I kept my hand in my pocket to conceal the weapon. The female officer holding his right arm started demanding something in Spanish, but the gunman continued to fight them. She repeated herself once more before the other deputy chimed in.

"Stop fighting us," he said.

The gunman continued to struggle.

"Stop resisting us!" the deputy demanded.

At this point, Sheriff Harding peaked out from behind a cracked door to catch a glimpse of what was happening. When he saw the struggle, he opened the door completely and stood in the doorway.

"Knock it off!" he yelled. His deep voice radiated throughout the main office. Whether he understood English or not, the gunman clearly got the idea. He stopped the hopeless struggle and complied with the officers. Everyone else quieted down for a second or two before Sheriff Harding disappeared into the office once more.

Next up, the pilot. Earlier, I'd thought he was the more reasonable one of them all. He'd seemed to have a handle on the situation aboard the plane. Now, I was second-guessing my earlier observation. Reality must've set in with him. This must've been his first crime. He was panicking as the deputies brought him into the lobby. The deputies seemed to be annoyed by his protests.

"I'm just the pilot," he stated. "I can't get into trouble for this, right?"

"Look," began a deputy, "just do what they say and you'll be fine."

"I can't go in there!" replied the pilot. "I haven't done anything. I've got kids." He recognized me. "Look!" He tried to point at me, his cuffs clanging. "Ask him! I tried to talk Chambon out of it. He knows I had nothing to do with this! Tell them!"

I didn't say anything. I just watched.

"Tell them!" he demanded again. "You all have to believe me!"

"Please calm down," pleaded the officer.

"Just ask him!" The pilot grabbed the deputy's arm as best he could and tried to shake him. "I can't go in there! I'm not like them!"

The pilot began to struggle with the deputies and jump around. The deputies, on the other hand, started to lose control as fear washed over the pilot like a potent drug. Another officer got up from behind the desk to offer assistance while they put the pilot flat on the floor.

"I'm getting tired of this," said one of the deputies. "Stop it!"

They helped the pilot back up after he calmed down some.

At this point, Sheriff Harding returned. "What the hell is going on?"

"We can't get him to calm down," said a deputy.

Sheriff Harding took a look at the pilot, who appeared like he was about to cry. The sheriff just shook his head. "Take him to the back and put him by himself. Don't let the others see this."

The deputies took him to the back as the pilot continued to resist. "I can't go back there!" he yelled repeatedly. "I'm not like them!"

A woman who appeared to be strung out on something and was waiting to be booked couldn't take the pilot anymore.

"Shut the hell up!" she yelled. "I can't take that pussy anymore!" She covered her ears like the sound of his voice was agonizing.

"Quiet!" yelled an officer.

The pilot's voice grew fainter as they disappeared in the back.

I looked around the room at the other characters in the office. There was a petty thief. The officers knew him by his first name; he must've been a regular. Another was a skinny man covered in tattoos. Even his shaved head was nothing but a giant tattoo. He looked like a drug dealer. He was scary to look at but impossible not to notice. How could you not look at him? I bet it would've taken ten minutes just to read him.

I couldn't help but admire the officers, even if I was on their wrong side at times. After witnessing the kind of people they dealt with each night, I couldn't help but ask myself, *Why would they want to do this job?* I was just glad they were on my side. Despite everything happening, they still seemed calm and collected and radiated a sense of strong will.

Will appeared from the back and entered the lobby. He was holding a file. "Colt," he began, "come on back with me."

I followed him toward the back; we passed the rooms where Chambon's crew were being booked. When we passed the kitchen, Will pointed with the file still in his hand. "There's some fresh coffee in there if you want some."

I eyed the coffee as I passed by it. Any other time, I would have poured a cup. It had become a staple ever since I went into business for myself. Caffeine was the least of my concerns now, though.

"No, thanks," I said.

Will opened a door and led me into a dark room with a large one-way mirror window. On the other side of the glass was Chambon, sitting at a table with a defeated look. Across from him sat Sheriff Harding with that signature stern look of his. He wasn't even fazed. It was enough to make anyone cringe.

"Tom's preparing to begin the interrogation," Will said. "I'm afraid we may not get much."

"He hasn't been talking?" I asked.

"No," he replied. "He's been quiet." Will flipped a switch next to a speaker to listen in on the conversation as we peered through the window.

"Can they hear us?" I asked.

"No," said Will. "I'm sure he knows we're here, though."

"Mr. Chambon," began Sheriff Harding, "you've been cooperative since we've brought you into custody. Maybe we can work something out."

Chambon looked down at the table, then back up at the sheriff.

"You're facing a lot of charges, you know," the sheriff continued. "If you tell me where Carina is, I bet I can work with the judge to drop some of these charges. Reduce your sentence."

Chambon looked to the side like he was considering the option, but he didn't say anything. He looked back at the sheriff.

"Where's Carina at?" Sheriff Harding asked.

Chambon didn't say anything.

"Is she still alive?" continued the sheriff.

Chambon still refused to answer.

Sheriff Harding sat back in his chair and folded his arms. His temper was escalating, though he tried his best to conceal it.

"This is pissing me off," I said. "I would like to go in there and ring Chambon's neck myself. I'll make him talk."

"Believe me, Colt," Will said, "Tom wants to do the same, but we have to follow the law." He got quiet for a minute before he continued. He shook his head in exasperation. "Chambon must still believe he has a good hand in this card game."

"Okay," Sheriff Harding continued. "You must think Carina is a trump card. A get-out-of-jail-free card. I can promise you, it's not going to work like that. I've got a team looking for that girl as we speak. One way or another, we will find her. And you can sit in prison and rot away thinking about the opportunity you missed right here on this very night."

He pointed down at the table with his index finger to add emphasis to the statement. He was still fighting to keep his cool. Still no response from Chambon. "Would you at least like to tell me why you did all this?"

Chambon gazed at the sheriff with a puzzled look.

"I know why you took Carina," the sheriff said. "That's not what I mean. You were worked up on that plane. You were stressed. That wasn't from my crew alone. Do you owe someone some money? Do you have another boss? What the hell, huh?"

Chambon looked away again.

"I wonder what's running through his mind right now," I said.

"A lot more than what he's telling us," Will replied.

"I think I'm going to wait for my lawyer," said Chambon. He looked up and smirked like an idea had struck him. Then he nodded his head in agreement. "Yeah, I'd rather wait for my lawyer."

Sheriff Harding's lips pressed into a thin line at the response. He looked like he was about to lose it, but he stopped himself. He lifted his hands and dropped them on the table.

"You have that right," he said. "But I warn you, Chambon. If something happens to Carina, you will be held responsible. If she dies—if she's not dead already—you will be charged for murder!"

Chambon's face changed. I could tell that last remark had rubbed him the wrong way. "I want my damn lawyer!" he replied.

"I heard you the first time!" said Sheriff Harding. He stood up and walked out of the room, slamming the door shut behind him.

"Did you guys find any clues as to where Carina might be?" I asked.

"No," Will replied. "They haven't found anything. Some of the deputies asked the neighbors if they saw anything. Not much came of it. You know how they are. They're quiet and just want to keep to themselves. We couldn't even find anyone with a security camera."

I could hear Sheriff Harding approaching the door from the other side. "I'd like to take that scrawny maggot out back, put my hands around him, and ring his neck. Damn little maggot!" The door swung open. The sheriff looked over at Will. "Did this creep's record come in yet?"

"I got it right here," Will replied. "Fresh from the New Orleans Police Department. It arrived just before you began talking with him. They keep tabs on this guy. They say he's a known con artist. Let's see what we're dealing with here." Will opened the file and began glancing over it. "Looks like he was born out on the streets in the Big Easy. A lot of petty crimes growing up. Probably trying to survive."

Will skimmed through the pages some more. "It looks like he stepped it up a bit when he got older. Started hanging around the business sector. He went to prison after he took some investors for a ride." He paused. "Listen to this: He managed to take funds from several investors claiming himself to be a mutual fund manager. He offered them a premium return. He then used the funds to move drugs out on the streets. He somehow used the port to move everything. He paid the investors their promised return and pocketed the rest. It looks like Customs finally caught on to his game."

"What happened when he got out of prison?" I inquired. "He left New Orleans in search of new territory?"

"Basically," Will replied. He skimmed the record some more. "It looks like he spends every dime he receives. Chambon's weakness is greed. Before he was arrested, he had a mansion, fast cars, you name it. But he barely had enough for a lawyer. They had to appoint one for him."

"And now he's working in Ocala," Sheriff Harding began. "Ripping off the rich people and turning our county upside down."

"What do we do now?" I asked.

"Wait for his damn lawyer," replied the sheriff.

"SHATTERED ARROWHEADS"

The fluorescent lights above gleamed off a glass case holding shattered arrowheads—relics of the tribes that once inhabited the local lands. It was one of the many relics displayed on Sheriff Harding's desk. They were fitting for a diehard 'Nole fan and alumni such as the sheriff.

The office was silent as we anxiously waited to hear from Chambon's defense attorney.

Sheriff Harding was standing behind his desk. He couldn't sit down. He was too worked up over the ordeal. He looked out the office window into the darkness. Will and I were sitting in the chairs in front of his desk, waiting to hear something. We didn't even talk to one another. A light knock at the door finally broke the uncomfortable silence.

"Come in," said Sheriff Harding. His deep voice radiated through the door. He turned when he heard the door handle move. Will and I turned to see who was entering. The opening door revealed an older man with a gray beard who was wearing a light-colored three-piece suit and brown wing tip shoes. I had seen him before. He looked much like you would expect any Southern lawyer to. He seemed very tired.

"Mr. Bailey?" Sheriff Harding asked. "I wasn't expecting to see you this late."

"It wasn't planned," the lawyer said. He took his time to pronounce every word properly with his elegant Southern accent.

"That Mr. Chambon is very particular. He turned down the first defense attorney. He didn't like the fact that he was from Ohio. He wanted someone that he could trust. He wanted a fellow Southerner." Bailey smiled as he closed the door behind him. "When I was told this, I had to meet this man myself."

"The guy's a two-faced bastard," replied Sheriff Harding. He was far blunter in the way he spoke compared to Bailey.

"All of my clients are innocent until proven guilty," Bailey said. "They are entitled to a fair trial even if they arise from, say, rambunctious parts of our community." He began to sit down in the chair near the door, then stopped. "May I?"

"Of course," said Sheriff Harding. He waved a hand toward the chair.

Bailey sat down and placed his briefcase on the floor next to him. "Besides, when I heard he kidnapped Carina, I wanted to do anything possible to get that girl back."

"Did he say anything?" I asked.

"Who's this man?" the lawyer asked as he looked up at Sheriff Harding.

"He's a pain-in-the-ass PI," the sheriff replied. "He's also Carina's boyfriend. I think she could do a lot better, myself."

I glanced at Sheriff Harding, a bit aggravated with that last remark. I managed to keep myself from saying anything.

"A PI, you say?" Bailey reached into his pocket and pulled out a gold case. He opened it, pulled out a business card, and handed it to me. "Just in case. You never know when you'll need a good lawyer." He put the case away before continuing. I looked at the card and put it in my wallet. "My client would like to make a deal."

"What kind of deal?" asked Sheriff Harding. I could tell he was hesitant.

"He will give us the location where he was holding Carina if we reduce his time to be served. I'll obviously work with the judge in the morning."

Sheriff Harding sat down in his chair and thought about the of-fer. He rubbed his face with one hand.

"We don't have much to go on, sir," Will said.

The sheriff didn't move a muscle apart from his eyes. He glanced right at Will before sitting back in his chair and clasping his hands across the armrest. "That's what I hate," he said. "I wish I had a way to verify this."

"I can check it out myself," I said.

"Rescue the girl and ride off into the sunset," Sheriff Harding stated. "Just like a cowboy, right? You know that's a great way to get yourself killed."

"I like this one," Bailey said, half laughing. "A modern-day John Wayne."

I didn't respond to any of the comments. I was just thinking of Carina.

"Get the location and we'll check it out," Sheriff Harding told Bailey. "If we get Carina or find some clues as to her whereabouts, we'll make a deal. That's the only way I'll make a deal with him. Be sure to remind Chambon of that last part."

"I'll get the location," Bailey replied. He stood up, grabbed his briefcase, and exited the room.

Sheriff Harding looked over at Will. "Let's round up the troops." Then he looked at me and pointed. "I know I can't stop you from coming, so let's have it out now. Don't you dare try any of that hero crap. Just let us do our job. I don't want anyone to get shot. You understand me?"

"I do," I said. I was getting aggravated with Sheriff Harding and biting my lip.

"I mean it, Colt," Sheriff Harding replied. "Don't get involved."

"I said I understand!" I said. Tensions were beginning to rise.

"Hey, hey, hey!" Will interjected. "Everyone needs to take it down a notch. This does not help Carina."

Sheriff Harding and I stared at one another for a second or two longer before he stood up.

"Just get everyone together," the sheriff said to Will. Then he walked out of the room.

"You can ride with me, Colt," Will said.

I exhaled for a second to release some of my anxiety. Will could tell I was worried. "It'll be okay. We'll get her back. I need you to come with me."

We both exited the room, and I followed Will into his office. He reached into a closet and pulled out a bulletproof vest. "Before we go, I want you to put this on. Considering the guys we're tangling with, we might get bloody."

Now with a definite location, a line of squad cars was on its way in the early morning hours. I sat in the passenger seat of Will's truck as we traveled to the location. It was about an hour away. We turned off the highway and onto another dirt road, which slowed our progress. I peered out the window and noted a small skulk of foxes in the headlights. They froze for a second, maybe two, before they quickly trotted out of the path of the vehicles and disappeared into the woods.

"Something's not right," I said. "I just have a feeling. I don't know why."

"Either way," Will said, "we still have to check it out." He got quiet for a minute. "Colt, this time, I want you to stay in the car until we tell you everything is okay. Understand?"

"I understand," I replied. I just continued to look out the window.

"I'll signal you when it's all clear. Got it?"

"I got it."

The line of cars stopped up ahead. Sheriff Harding started talking over the radio.

"I see the location up ahead," he began. "It looks like an old metal garage of some sort. It's completely fenced off, except for a tight front entrance. No gate. If there's anyone there, they probably already saw our headlights. They know something's up. We're just going to swarm it. Just circle the building. I want you guys in the back to block the entrance with your car. I'll give the signal."

"Remember what I said, Colt," Will stated. "Just stay in here—we got it."

"Let's move in!" Sheriff Harding yelled over the radio.

The light bars atop the cars came to life in unison, lighting the woods with strobes of red and blue. The column of cars and trucks hurried into the facility and split in two as they began to circle around all sides of the building. The drivers aimed the front of their cars at the structure. The officers then exited their vehicles and took cover behind the open doors with guns drawn.

Will entered the facility and swung his truck around. I held on to a handle above the door and the center console so that I didn't fly out of my seat. Will slammed on the brakes, then quickly put the car in park. We were facing an old door on the side of the building.

"Get down, Colt."

Will swung open the door and assumed the same position as the others. I got down in my seat but kept my head high enough to just see over the dash. I scanned everything. Every exit to the building was covered. The last car pulled in and blocked the entrance to ensure no one would escape. A few seconds went by before I heard Sheriff Harding yell over a bullhorn.

"The building is surrounded. Come out with your hands up."

I looked back at the building. It just stood silent. No lights, no movements, nothing from inside.

"Come out with your hands up," Sheriff Harding continued. "Keep them where we can see them."

Everyone waited patiently. The officers were eager to see who was going to come out first.

"I'm going to give you thirty more seconds to comply," Sheriff Harding said as one final warning. "If you do not comply, we're coming in." After the allotted time passed, he spoke into his radio. "Will, I want you guys to go in first."

No explanation was needed. Will and two deputies moved toward the door in front of the truck. I could see their figures hurrying across the lot in the medley of spotlights and dancing red and blue strobe lights. One was carrying a battering ram. Will and the other officer acted as backup with guns drawn. The old door didn't stand a chance. One strike and it swung open like it was about to fall off the hinges. The deputy with the battering ram stood back while Will and the other officer hurried inside.

I glanced around. Everyone was waiting for the next signal. I looked over at Sheriff Harding. After about a minute, he gave the go-ahead for everyone else to move in quickly. I decided it was safe enough to sit up in my seat to get a better look. Another minute went by before I started seeing windows in the building light up one by one. No gunshots either—a great sign. After about five minutes, I saw Will appear in the doorway. He began waving me over. I exited the truck and limped over to the entrance as quickly as possible.

"Colt, be careful where you step."

"Any sign of Carina?" I asked.

"No, she's not here. I want you to come in and take a look around. We need you to see if you recognize anything."

I walked through the door, which led to what looked like an old break room. There were a couple of cheap tables and chairs and an old coffeepot. It was filthy. Will led me through the room to a door located on the opposite side. That door opened to a large garage and a disturbing sight. Scattered across the floor were three dead bodies and hundreds of brass bullet casings.

"Watch your step," Will said. I looked down; there was a casing near my foot. "This whole place is a crime scene."

"I know this place," I said. "This is where I was taken earlier to-day." I looked around the room. "There was a Lincoln parked over here, and the SUV they had me in entered through this garage door." I saw a chair in the corner. "I think that's the chair they tied me to. It was out in the middle of the floor about here." I pointed at the spot.

"It looks like all hell broke loose not long after they took you back to town," Will said.

"Colt," said Sheriff Harding. He waved me over. "Come over here. Watch your step." I walked over to the first body. "Look down as his face without disturbing the body." I kneeled to take a closer look. "Do you recognize him?"

"No," I said. "He wasn't with Chambon earlier."

We repeated the process with the other two bodies. The result was the same. I didn't recognize any of them.

"I wonder if Chambon was running from these guys or if they were working for him," I thought out loud.

"He knows a lot more than what he's saying," said Sheriff Harding.

"You think this is a deal gone bad?" asked Will.

"It could be," the sheriff replied. "Or Chambon could be on someone else's turf."

~ 16 ~

"I GUESS THE MAN HAS A PLAN."

The white ceiling lights of Sheriff Harding's office beat down on our heads. A feeling of defeat lingered in the room. We found ourselves in the same position as before. There were no clues as to the whereabouts of Carina. Just more unanswered questions.

We were all silent. We could not help but wonder if Carina was even alive. I started to gaze out the window, which I often did when I was contemplating something. I was thinking about what we knew. If there was anything we may have missed, something we thought might have been unimportant. I stared at the church across the street. I looked at the large crucifix in the front, lit among the darkness by a floodlight just before dawn.

A light knock at the door broke the silence.

"Come in," said Sheriff Harding. He was sitting down this time. Even his voice wasn't as vibrant as before.

The door opened. It was Bailey again. He didn't bother sitting down. He stayed in the doorway. I could tell he knew he wasn't going to like Sheriff Harding's response to what he had to say. "My client says he has another location for you to check."

"Are you kidding me?" Sheriff Harding began. "Chambon's in more trouble now than he was before. We don't have any sign of Carina, and he has three dead bodies to account for. The governor's probably going to sign his death warrant." Bailey got quiet and looked down. "I'm not going on another fool's errand. I can't keep taking all of these deputies away from their posts."

"I understand," Bailey replied. "I'm going to be here until the hearing. Let me know what you want to do." He exited the room.

"I wonder what Chambon is hiding," said Will.

"I think he wants to stay in jail for now," I said. They both looked at me like I was crazy. "I think he knew Carina wasn't at that garage all along. He knew about the bodies too. And whatever happened there earlier. I think it scared him. That's why he was so tense on the jet. Someone is still looking for him."

"So, you're saying Chambon sent us to find those bodies," said Sheriff Harding. "He wanted to rack up more incriminating evidence so he could stay in jail."

"That's a bet I would take," I said.

"That makes sense," Will said. He started talking while moving one of his hands around in the air. "There was a kid, I remember, arrested for robbing a store. It wasn't much; it was a petty theft, and he was allowed to go. Thing is, he didn't want to go. He wanted to stay in jail." He leaned forward for more emphasis. "It turns out, the store owner had a bad temper, and this kid had convinced himself that the store owner was out to get him."

"That was a dumb kid, though," said Sheriff Harding.

"He didn't know any better," Will replied. "But that's not my point. He was afraid to leave because he thought the store owner wanted to hurt him. He never did, obviously. The real question here is, How bad is this guy that Chambon is running from?"

Sheriff Harding sat back in his chair and thought about the conversation, twirling a pencil in his fingers.

"Alright," he said. "If that little bastard wants to play games with us, we can play games with him. I think I have an idea to make him talk." He thought some more before continuing. "The judge might be able to help us out. What I'm going to suggest is risky, but this is for Carina."

"What are you going to do?" I asked.

"You'll see at Chambon's hearing," Sheriff Harding replied. He stood up and looked at Will. "Do me a favor. Have a couple officers check out that other location. See if they find anything."

"I'll have it taken care of," Will said.

Sheriff Harding hurried out the door. Will and I both looked at one another, unsure of what idea had suddenly entered the sheriff's head.

"I guess the man has a plan," Will said.

~ 17 ~

"A REHABILITATED MAN"

The tension in the front row of the court was easy to sense. Most of the defendants had been sitting in the lobby of the sheriff's office the night before. Now, they waited apprehensively for the judge to enter the room. As they all awaited their fates, everyone else in the room sat silently. The atmosphere was only broken by the occasional cough or door opening. Then, there were footsteps as someone entered the room.

"All rise," said an officer. The judge finally entered through a door at the front of the court and sat down at the bench. Everyone in the room followed suit and sat, following proper courtroom procedures.

I sat in the back with Will at my side. I was eager to see what Sheriff Harding had in store for Chambon. The court began the proceedings so they could get started for the day.

"We should find out Tom's plan pretty quick," Will said quietly, careful not to disturb anyone around us.

"How do you know that?" I slightly turned my head without taking my eyes off the judge. I spoke quietly as well.

"Chambon's up first," he replied.

The judge began looking through his stack of files.

"Who do we have first?" the judge asked the officer. The microphone picked up the quiet chat between them.

"We have Mr. Chambon," the officer replied.

The judge sorted through the files until he found Chambon's. He began scanning through it while he talked. The whole thing looked more like a show than a serious proceeding.

"Mr. Chambon," the judge began, "you're not a very nice man based on what I'm reading. I see you even did some time in Louisiana."

"Your Honor," said Mr. Bailey. "That has no relevance here."

"Just curious," said the judge. "What brings you to our humble little town?"

Mr. Bailey and the judge began going over the charges.

"Shame, shame," said the judge. He got quiet for a moment as he examined the file some more before placing it down on his desk.

"In light of your time served in Louisiana," he began, "I'm going to assume you are a rehabilitated man. I'm also going to assume that bad elements of your past caught up with you this time while trying to live a rehabilitated man's life. It happens at times when trying to start anew."

The look on Chambon's face was one of shock. The same could be said for the prosecutor's.

"You can't be serious," said the prosecutor. "Just look what he's involved in, Your Honor."

"Mr. Chambon," the judge continued, "I'm going to release you. We will set a date for your first court appearance sometime in November. You will, of course, be required to appear in person. Does that time frame work for the defense?"

The look on Bailey's face was one of disbelief and happiness. He put his hands out like he didn't know what to say. "Of course, Your Honor," he said with a smile. He dropped his hands to the desk in front of him. He turned to his client and shook his hand as a sign of congratulations, like they had won the first round.

Chambon was still in disbelief as to what was happening.

"Your Honor," he said. He stood up and extended his right hand out toward the judge. "Are you sure you looked at everything in that file?"

"Mr. Bailey," said the judge, "I advise you to talk to your client."

Bailey managed to sit Chambon back down in his chair.

"What are you doing?" Mr. Bailey asked. "Most people in your position go to jail without bail. Be glad."

"Your Honor!" continued Chambon.

"Be quiet, Chambon!" said Bailey.

An officer began leading Chambon out of the courtroom.

"Do you think this is a wise decision?" Chambon continued. The officer finally managed to drag him out of the room, with Bailey in pursuit.

Will and I left the courtroom and returned to Sheriff Harding's office.

"Well," Will began, "he's out free. What do we do now?"

"We just wait," Sheriff Harding replied. "Let's see how desperate Chambon is. If he wants off the streets, he's going to approach one of us. He'll tell us everything he knows."

"How long do you think we'll have to wait?" I asked.

"He'll probably approach one of us today. If someone is looking for him, they're watching Chambon right now. He knows it, too. He'll want to get to safety as soon as possible. Until then, we just have to wait."

"Colt," Will said. "He's right. We've done everything we can for now. There's no point in waiting around here. You should head back home."

"He has a point," Sheriff Harding said. "You look like the walking dead. You need to get some rest."

"I can't sleep," I replied.

"We may need you again," the sheriff said. "It's best if you're rested up by then. We all need some rest. You could cut the tension between us with a knife. We need a break from this." We all got quiet. Sheriff Harding could tell I didn't want to leave. "When Chambon makes contact with one of us, you'll be the first person I call, okay?" I exhaled and nodded my head in agreement. "But I expect the same from you," he continued. "If he approaches you, you contact us immediately, okay?"

I just looked at the sheriff.

$$\sim 18 \sim$$

"I BET YOU'D LOOK FOR A WAY OUT, TOO."

The water tower was coming into view as my truck approached Williston. The afternoon sun was obscured by scattered cloud cover. I could not predict whether it was going to rain or whether the sun was going to shine.

My truck hummed along on the way back to my office as I continued to cross-examine the events in my head. I was hoping for some new clues. Any new clue. Any sign as to Carina's whereabouts. Anything at this point. I turned the corner, entered the parking lot behind my place, and backed my truck into its usual spot. Then I limped through the back door, stopped, and took in my surroundings. Duke and I had such a comfortable place. It was modest but homey. Now it was a disaster.

I inspected the damage done by Chambon's crew. Aside from the contents of the drawers and closets being scattered everywhere, some pieces had just been unnecessarily destroyed. That had been done deliberately. My pendulum clock stood silent thanks to a sharp impact marked by a web of scratches stretching across the glass. Duke's bed had been cut open with a knife; cotton was scattered all over the floor. My mattress and some of the furniture were cut up as well. I wandered around some more before looking into the mirror I had hanging in the hallway. I saw my reflection staring back at me through the shattered glass.

I hobbled to the front office and looked around. It was in much the same shape. Some of the glass in the display cases had been broken, and some of the relics were missing. My desk drawers had been ransacked and some of the furniture turned upside down. My old wooden desk had probably been too heavy for them to lift; otherwise, they would have turned that upside down as well. I stopped and looked around, trying to figure out where to start before limping over to the windows and opening the blinds to let some light in. I began flipping over some of the chairs. Then I heard the front door open.

"Need some help?" said a voice.

I turned and saw Keke in the doorway.

"I got it, Keke. Thank you." I went back to picking up my office.

Keke helped himself inside and shut the door behind him. "I was thinking about our case."

"Keke, not now. I have no idea where Carina's at, my stomach is in a tight knot, and I feel like strangling someone. I don't want to hear one more thing about this case."

He didn't even hear me. "I was thinking if I was the bad guy. You know, I put myself in his shoes. Where would I hide Carina?"

"Keke, how do you know about Carina?"

"The whole town probably knows by now."

"Figures."

"Anyway, what if I wanted to hide Carina? It would have to be in a place where she'd be secure. A place where no one could find her or have access to her, but *I* would need to have easy access to her. I would also need to have the ability to move her on short notice when it came time to exchange her."

"Keke." I shook my head. "Not now. I'm fed up with the whole thing."

"I would take Carina outside the country. Like to Cuba or the Gulf. Not far. Just distant enough where I could get my hands on her when I needed her. Think about it: We're surrounded by water.

The Caribbean is full of countries easily accessible by a short flight. What could the authorities do? It's outside their jurisdiction."

I turned another one of my chairs right side up and sat down in it. I thought about his words.

"Then," Keke continued, "when it was time to turn over Carina, I would come in somewhere that no one would expect but that was easy to leave from on short notice. I would want a place that's deceptive. Is that the correct word?" I nodded my head in agreement. "Not like those abandoned warehouses and places you see in the movies. It's too cliché."

We were silent for a few seconds. I was thinking about what Keke had said. "That makes a lot of sense, Keke. But it also scares me. That means it's going to be even harder to find Carina. Where did you learn all this stuff?"

"I watch TV."

"Where?"

"At the train depot."

"They let you stay there?"

"In a manner of speaking."

"What do you mean?"

He paused for a little bit and looked down at the floor. Then he looked back up at me. "I've got to go!"

"Where are you going?" I put my hands out.

"I just got to go." He turned and began to hurry out the door.

"Keke, I'm not going to tell anybody. I was just curious." I stood up and followed him out the door.

By the time I was outside, he had already disappeared around the corner. I felt kind of bad. I hadn't meant to chase him off. I'd just stumbled upon the discovery. I hadn't known he was staying at the depot. I decided there was nothing else I could do, headed back inside, and shut the door. This time, I made sure it was locked and latched the chain guard. I went back to picking up my office. Then I heard footsteps slowly approaching from down the hall.

"Keke," I said. "What are you doing? Today's not the day to play games."

I turned to look at him, then stopped. I couldn't believe my eyes. It was Chambon. He was standing in the hall.

He didn't say a word. He looked more worried than anything else.

I couldn't contain myself. I forgot about whatever it was that I had in my hand. I threw it on the floor and lunged at Chambon, grabbing him by the shirt collar.

"Colt! Wait!" He put his hands up like he didn't want to fight. I picked him up off his feet and threw him across my desk. He slid across the top and landed on the floor on the other side. I had no idea where I'd found the strength to do that. I had lost track of everything around me except for Chambon.

He began pleading with me. "I know! I know!" He kept putting his hands up. "You're upset about that girl!"

"You're damn straight, Chambon! Where's Carina?" I grabbed him by the collar again and slung him against the wall. "Where is she?" I slammed him into the wall again. "Damn it, Chambon! You better start talking!"

"Stop!" yelled Chambon. It didn't help. I continued to threaten him. "Stop! If you stop, I'll tell you everything I know!"

I was breathing heavily. I wanted to throw him around the room some more, but I managed to get myself under control. I let go of his shirt, and he closed his eyes for a second to catch his breath. I couldn't help it. I balled my fist and punched his nose. He grabbed his face and doubled over. Then I put the tips of my index and middle fingers in his nostrils and dragged him off to my toolshed. I opened the door, led him in, and shut it behind me. I turned over a chair and sat him down in it, facing the window. While he was recovering, I opened the blinds to let some more light into the room. Then I opened my safe, pulled out my Colt revolver, and resecured it. I sat down in a chair opposite him, by the window. I could see blood running down his face. I pointed the gun right at him.

"This is a .45 Colt, Chambon. I promise I can do a lot of damage before you kick off. Now, you better tell me everything you know."

"You going to shoot me?" he asked.

"Chambon, there are many things I would like to do to you right now. Believe me, this is one of the nicer ones." Chambon wiped some of the blood from his face and carefully felt at his nose. "I want to know what's going on and I want to know right now. No more games."

"I want to make a deal," he said.

"No," I replied bluntly. "You tell me everything you know. Then we'll discuss a deal."

"The alternative?" he said.

"You're looking at it."

"Willing to commit murder?" he asked. I could tell he was starting to calm down. He was reverting back to his sly ways.

"Take a look around, Chambon. I'll just tell them it was a struggle and I had no choice."

He started to reach into his jacket. I lifted the gun higher, ready for whatever he was about to pull out.

"Relax, Colt." Chambon removed a handkerchief from his suit jacket. "I just want to stop the blood that's gushing from my nose thanks to you." He wiped his nose, then held the cloth tight against it. He inhaled a couple of times before beginning. "I work for a man named Moreno. You ever heard of him?"

"No," I replied. "The name doesn't mean anything to me."

"He's a drug lord in South America. I don't know where his empire is located exactly. I'm on a need-to-know basis with him. He used to have a big market here in Florida back in the seventies. It was easier for him to move around back then. He used to come in through Cedar Key. Great idea when you think about it. Sleepy little town along the water. Who would know?"

"And then the eighties came," I interjected.

"That's right," he replied. "Ole Ronny went to work on the drug runners. Moreno was forced to leave. There's still a reward for him you know. A handsome sum. God only knows how many murders he's wanted for."

"I don't care," I said. "You keep talking about the past. I want to know about the present."

"Moreno sat back and concentrated on smaller markets during the eighties. He kept his empire intact while his competition started to suffer. They tried so hard to hold on to their American markets that they made themselves targets."

"Now Moreno wants back in," I said. "He must feel that his competition is wiped out."

"That's right," Chambon replied. "He's an old man, but he's still greedy. I met him via one of his runners who was doing time in Louisiana. Moreno put me right to work as soon as I got out. He wanted to try some new ideas to penetrate the markets here in Florida."

"Which were?"

"He asked me to travel to Ocala and scout for anyone who would be willing to traffic goods for a high return."

"By using their horses as mules," I said.

"That right," Chambon said. "We wanted to see if customs would overlook it. And they did."

"So, you used Tempest for your dirty work. I'm surprised about Mrs. Philippe. I thought she was sincere."

"That old woman didn't give a rat's ass about that horse! She jumped at the chance when I offered it to her. Her husband died of cancer, and he donated most of his fortune to medical research. He was actually a very good man. He left her a considerable amount and his prized mare." He looked to the side and lifted his eyebrows. "I would have taken it." Then he looked back at me. "But it wasn't enough for her."

"She was greedy," I said.

"Right, but I was too," he replied. I just shook my head in disgust. "I picked up the horse with my own crew without her knowing."

"Skimming off the top," I said.

"I would have disappeared, too, if she hadn't panicked. She managed to find out the horse was missing. That was when she began worrying about Moreno. She knew we couldn't go to the police, but she wanted to find Tempest. I couldn't risk that. So, I started asking around."

"And that's when you found my information," I said.

"I gave your info to Mrs. Philippe, and she was content. I figured I had bought myself plenty of time to do my part." He looked down at the floor and wiped his nose again. His white button-down shirt was covered in fresh blood. "I honestly thought you were just some dumb redneck. I figured you would either not catch on or just give up."

"Chambon," I began. I took a deep breath and exhaled. "You are a sick son of a bitch. You know that? Look at everything you've done."

"If you'd raised yourself on the streets of Algiers, I bet you'd look for a way out, too."

We both paused for a few minutes.

I finally broke the silence. "Where's Carina?"

Chambon hesitated. "I don't know," he said lightly. He looked down at the floor.

"What?"

"I don't know."

"What do you mean you don't know!" I demanded.

"I think Moreno might have her," he said delicately. I could feel my blood pressure rising. Everything around me seemed to just blur. All my attention was fixed on Chambon. "I took her to the garage and left before Moreno hit it. I think his crew has her. They are still looking for me."

"Chambon," I said calmly. I checked my revolver, stood up, and secured it in my belt next to my buckle. Then I walked over to him. He looked up at me. "Chambon, that's the wrong answer!" I grabbed him by the shirt collar and started shaking him. He kicked the chair out from under himself. "Where's Carina! Where's Moreno!"

I stopped shaking him, and he fell on his knees.

He put his arms out like he wanted to surrender. "Colt, please!"

I got a tighter hold on his shirt collar before threatening him again. "Damn you, Chambon! Answer me!"

Glass shattered behind me. Within a half second, Chambon was jerked out of my arms and thrust across the room.

~ 19 ~

"I'M ONLY GIVING YOU A SMALL TASTE."

Chambon's body was leaning against the wall, motionless. One shot in the head had taken him from our world, along with all his secrets. Ironically, as one door closed, another opened: The sun drifted out from behind the clouds, lighting the room.

I was fazed for a moment. I looked around the room for a second before I realized what had happened. I found myself lying flat on the floor. I looked over at Chambon's body sitting against the wall. I looked over at the shattered window and crawled below it to stay out of the line of fire. Whoever had fired the shot was using a silencer. I reached up, closed the blinds, and stayed low. Another few seconds went by before Chambon's phone began to ring to some Cajun melody.

I hesitated for a second or two to gather the courage to move out of my spot. I finally got up and walked over to Chambon's body, but I stayed low. I don't know why. It was probably just the excitement of the situation. The shooter couldn't see through the blinds. I reached into his pocket, pulled out the phone, and answered it.

"Colt?" said the voice. It sounded like an older man with a Spanish accent. His English was well pronounced. I was quiet at first. I was trying to figure out if I recognized the voice. "Is this Colt?"

"This his him," I said hesitantly.

"This is Moreno," he replied. I remained quiet. "Are you there?"

127

"I am," I said.

"Relax, Colt," he said. "If I wanted you dead, you would be dead now. I shot Chambon for both our sakes."

"What do you want?" I asked.

"It's what *you* want," he replied. "That's what you need to be thinking. It's simply what you want." I stayed quiet. "I know two of my bags are with the police," he continued. "I don't care about those any more. At this point, I just want to recover what I can. Chambon really screwed up my plans."

"You want me to bring you the two remaining bags," I said.

"That's correct," he replied. "And in return, I'll give you that little spitfire Carina."

"Moreno, I need some proof. Chambon has done nothing but send us in circles. You guys shot that garage up pretty good. How do I know if she's even alive?"

"Colt!" yelled Carina.

"Carina!" I said.

"Just do as they say," she said.

"Carina! Wait!"

"That's it," Moreno said. "I'm only giving you a small taste. If you want the rest, you listen to me."

"What do you want me to do, Moreno?" I stood up from the floor and started pacing.

"Have you ever heard of Live Oak Key? It's along the coast near Cedar Key."

"I know exactly where that's at," I replied. "I used to fish around there as a kid."

"Good," he said. "Fond childhood memories. Meet me there at midnight. I'll find you. No police, no boats, nothing. Just bring me what's left of my shipment."

"Moreno, wait, I might need more time."

"No tricks, either. If I even suspect anything is wrong, I swear I'll cut this girl's throat out right in front of you. Then I'll make your last moments on earth the most miserable you've ever been before I send you back to God."

"Wait, Moreno!"

He hung up. I looked down at the phone. It was another burner. I placed it in my pocket and thought about my options. He was clearly watching me somehow. If I went to the police, he'd know. He'd kill Carina for sure. If I did as he said, there was a chance he'd still kill Carina and then me after he got the shipment. I weighed my options. I had to move fast. The clock was ticking, and the sun was setting.

I'm running out of time, I thought to myself. I looked around the room and noticed my holster belt lying on the floor. I took it as a sign. *I'm going to have to do this myself.*

I picked it up, opened the safe, and loaded cartridges into the empty slots. Then I opened my revolver, checked the cylinder to ensure each of the slots was loaded, then secured the gun in its holster. I opened my safe wider and looked at my other weapons. I decided to bring my carbine as well. Just in case. I shut the door to the safe and threw the belt over my right shoulder. Then I grabbed my knife, spurs, and other riding gear.

I headed out the back door and limped over to my truck. I opened the rear door to the cab, lifted the bench, and placed everything on the floor before slamming the door shut.

As I stood in the doorway of my toolshed, I gazed around the room one more time to ensure there was nothing else I needed. Chambon's cold face stared at the floor, his mouth hanging open.

"I'll contact Sheriff Harding about you later," I said out loud. Then I shut the door behind me and began making my way to Carina's.

Hold on, Carina, I thought. *Just a little longer. I'm on my way.*

~ 20 ~

"WE HAVE A JOB TO DO."

The setting sun was obscured by passing clouds as night approached. The headlights of the truck illuminated dust blowing around in the strong breeze as I rolled through the town. Shop owners were turning out their lights and closing up for the day. The turn at the water tower was marked by many lighted homes occupied by families unaware of the events unfolding among them—events many would never want associated with them, their community, and, most of all, their children.

I turned the corner and made my way down the gravel road I had become so familiar with over the past couple of days. Driving here was almost second nature now. Just by the rhythm of my hands on the steering wheel, I knew every bump, every pothole, and every imperfection. When I turned at the end of the property, I made my way to the pump house. I parked the truck, lit up the shed using the headlights, and exited the cab.

The wind was getting stronger and kicking up more dust. The weather was changing. I heard Levi in his pen. He was trotting along the perimeter of it, breaking the routine with each strong gust of wind. He would rear and buck, then stand defiantly on his hind legs at the center of his pen. The dark Cracker horse was unsettled, and he wanted out. Well, he was going to get his chance. Other horses in the facility took note of Levi's actions, and they couldn't help but neigh at his stress.

While Levi continued to grow unsettled, I staggered my way to the pump house, turned on a light, and grabbed the shovel I'd used earlier. Then I saw a red Coleman lantern hanging above me. I reached up and shook it. I was in luck. It still had fuel. I placed it on the bench and found a lighter. I pumped the lantern a few times and turned the knob. I could hear the gas flowing smoothly. With one strike of the lighter, the lantern came to life to light my way in the pump house.

The structure was undisturbed. I hung the lantern back above my head and went to work pulling back the gravel covering my hiding spot, then the dirt. I was careful not to puncture either of the bags. After a minute, I could see the wrapping of the first bag shining in the light. I used my hands to carefully wipe off the rest of the dirt and lift the bag. Then, I repeated the procedure with the other bag and wiped them both clean. I turned out the lantern, headed out the door, and carefully secured the drugs in my saddlebags.

Levi continued to grow restless. He was shaking his head around. I latched on my horse trailer and made sure everything was secure. Then I circled around and backed it toward Levi's pen. He was trotting around the perimeter of the fence again. He knew we were up to something. He was ready. I exited the truck and opened the rear door on the trailer. Then I opened his gate.

"Come on, Levi. We have a job to do."

Levi circled around the pen again, frustrated, before trotting out of the gate and right into the trailer. I secured him in place before tacking him up. I didn't want to dawdle when we arrived. Time was of the essence. Once Levi was ready, I exited the trailer, turned out the light, and secured the door.

There was one more thing that had to be taken care of before I left. I made my way to the cab and pulled out my flashlight. Then I began examining the undercarriage of my truck. It took me about five minutes, but I finally found the tracker a deputy had placed on my vehicle. I wasn't going to risk it. Moreno seemed to be more on top of things than Chambon. I couldn't imagine him not being prepared for something like this. I looked over the tracker quickly, then tossed it. I watched it disappear into the tall grass that was waving back and forth in the breeze.

I took one more look around the facility before climbing into the cab. The wind continued to pick up, and the moon was rising. The ringing of church bells began sounding from town in the distance.

It was time.

~ 21 ~

"ANOTHER DECEPTION"

The long road to the small coastal town of Cedar Key seemed to be as straight as an arrow and endless. The headlights of my truck revealed tall grass along both sides of the road waving in the breeze from the Gulf. On any other night, the breeze would have been a welcoming respite from the humid, sticky weather further inland. In the distance, the night sky revealed a storm brewing off the coast. Lightning bolts danced around one another as the thunderclouds approached.

My truck hummed along the highway as I approached Cedar Key. The road was empty. I looked in my rearview mirror and saw only the running lights of my horse trailer following behind in the darkness. The town was situated on a large island connected to the mainland by a bridge that ran to several other islands that dotted the area. Fortunately for me, I would not have to drive into town. I'd just stay on the mainland, on the outskirts of town, out of sight.

Just on the edge of town, I found a makeshift pullout for my truck and trailer. The headlights from my truck revealed two rows of bare dirt in the grass where cars had parked previously. I slowed my rig down and pulled into the area before parking. Then I crawled out of the cab. At first glance, the place didn't look like much. The area seemed to be overgrown, except for a high spot in the distance. Then I saw the historic sign across the street by another makeshift pullout. Tourists must have been stopping here in the daylight to take pictures by the marker. This was an old stop along the Florida Railroad that connected Cedar Key to Fernand-ina. The trains used the stop here to take on water and wood so they could finish the trip into town.

Levi kicked inside the trailer. He was ready to get out and get to work. I took another look around. I didn't see any traffic, and I was parked far enough from the road that I figured my rig would be okay. I might get a ticket, but that would be a small price to pay.

I limped around back, opened the trailer, and led Levi out. It was dark. This wasn't like town. There were no streetlights out here, hardly any homes. We were on our own. I double-checked my gear just to ensure I had everything. Levi was tacked up properly. My guns were loaded. And most importantly, I had Moreno's pack-ages.

I closed up the trailer and mounted Levi. I was ready to make my way across the street when I heard something moving in the shrubbery behind us. It stopped for a second when Levi and I looked in its direction. I couldn't believe my eyes. I had to look twice. I wasn't sure, but I thought I saw the outline of a Florida black wolf. The figure disappeared as quickly as it had appeared. Perhaps it was just as surprised by our presence. Either way, I couldn't help but think to myself, *Maybe there's hope yet.*

After we crossed the street, Levi and I disappeared into a grove of pine trees and palmettos with only the moonlight to guide us on our journey to Live Oak Key. The breeze was welcoming, but the smell was not. I didn't need to see to tell that the tide was out. In a way, it helped serve as a guide. The stronger the smell, the closer we were to the coast.

In some places, the brush seemed to be very thick. No problem for a Cracker horse like Levi. His breed had grown accustomed to moving cattle through the thick brush of South Florida. They'd been able to adapt to the harsh environment so much better than other breeds. Levi was a trooper. He pushed through the brush like a bulldozer making a path. I saw the look in his eyes. He was like me at this point: determined.

Eventually, I stopped Levi and dismounted. I was trying to get my bearings. I had never gone to Live Oak Key from the mainland before. Honestly, I wasn't even sure if I would be able to get near it. I knew the key was more like a small peninsula, but the whole area was a mixture of marshland and sawgrass dotted with palmettos and scrub oak. I looked up at the stars. I guess I was hoping for some guidance. I could hear the tide from the Gulf, and the smell was getting worse. I remounted and directed Levi forward.

"Come on, Levi. It's got to be this way."

The purple glow of lightning off in the distance was putting on a spectacular show as it stretched across the sky, almost as if it were reaching out a hand above our heads. Meanwhile, the wind continued to blow the sawgrass and cattails back and forth in a slow motion that almost seemed chilling and dreamlike. I kept my head low and pulled down my hat, and we continued forward. I wasn't sure what to expect.

After about thirty more minutes of what seemed like limitless wandering around in the woods, we finally found it. It was Live Oak Key. The weather in the distance may have been rough, but the skies above us were clear. It was midnight under a full high moon. I could just make out the outline of the island in the light. The problem was, we had gone as far as we could. The rest of it seemed like marsh. There was no way we could go any further.

"I hope they can find us," I said to Levi. "Otherwise, this whole thing was for naught." Levi looked at me, then started looking around like he was taking in his surroundings. "I guess all we can do now is wait."

I gazed at the key.

Live Oak Key always appeared to be a relaxing place. I had taken a kayak around here many times and fished to get my mind off things. It was a place I always looked forward to visiting. I would have never guessed that such a tranquil place could have two sides. My first glance had been misleading. Then again, why not? Given everything that had happened over the past two days, why shouldn't this place be anything but another deception?

A few more minutes went by before I noticed a few lights appear in the distance along the horizon of the Gulf. They were just off the coast, in the direction of the bad weather. It was a boat of some kind. It must have just entered US waters. After a few minutes, a smaller light appeared to rise above the deck and begin approaching. Then I heard a chopping noise. It was a helicopter. As it approached, the pilot turned on a spotlight and began scanning the coast. It had to be Moreno. He was looking for me. Levi was unsettled by the noise. I grabbed his reins and started petting his nose to calm him down. All the while, the helicopter continued to get closer.

Once the helicopter was near, I took my Stetson off and waved it in the air. No sooner had I done that than the spotlight turned on me and the helicopter approached. It hovered in the air for a few seconds before spinning around and scanning the area around me with the light. I placed my Stetson back on my head. Eventually, the pilot found a patch of high ground free of trees and slowly brought the aircraft down, careful not to hit anything with the blades. Levi started to shake his head and pull back, yanking me back along with him as the helicopter descended. I spun around and pulled tight on the reins as he continued to pull back. I leaned back on the balls of my feet—not that I could have stopped the large animal from darting away. It was more of a threat. It was a struggle with my limp, but I managed to calm the horse down.

"Come on, Levi. It's okay."

The Cracker horse calmed some. I turned back around and began to approach the helicopter with Levi in tow. The helicopter had landed and was pointing the spotlight in our direction. He was hard to see at first with the light in my eyes, but a tall man stepped out of the craft with two gunmen behind him. As I approached, I could make out more details. The tall man was wearing luxury clothing and had a completely shaved head. He appeared to be an older man, but he was in very good physical shape, with a large upper body. Not surprising, given his occupation. The man approached with the two gunmen following at his sides. They would not leave his sight.

"Are you Moreno?" I yelled. I had to raise my voice over the chopping sound of the helicopter. The blades were still spinning to make for a quick getaway.

"That is correct," I heard him say back with a Spanish accent. "You must be Colt."

He stepped closer to take a look. His gunmen kept a close eye on me. Moreno began laughing. "You must think you're John Wayne!" The other two laughed. "I want you to take that revolver and lift it out of the holster with your thumb and finger on the handle." I did as he requested. "Now toss it over here."

I followed the command and tossed my revolver to the dirt in front of him. Moreno picked it up and looked at me. "What else would a cowboy carry?"

"Do you have Carina?" I yelled.

"I guess the cowboy always wants to get the girl in the end!" he said. There was some more laughter before he yelled something in Spanish. Two more gunmen exited the helicopter. In between them was a girl with a sack on her head. The gunmen brought her to Moreno. He reached over, lifted the sack off her head, and put his hand out like she was on display. It was Carina.

"Carina!" I yelled.

Carina closed her eyes for a minute so they could adjust. "Colt!" she said.

Moreno handed my gun to one of the gunmen and grabbed Carina by the shirt collar. "Do you have what's left of my shipment?" he yelled. The gunmen that had brought Carina over propped their weapons on their shoulders and stepped back. The first pair of gunmen pointed their weapons in my direction.

I put my hands up in the light as a signal for them to wait. I slowly stepped backward toward Levi. The gunmen continued to follow me with the barrels of their guns.

"No tricks!" yelled Moreno.

I reached into the satchels, pulled out both drug bags, and lifted them into the air in both hands.

"Bring them here!" Moreno yelled.

I began walking back toward the helicopter, then stopped. Moreno was eyeing the shipment. He let go of Carina and began to approach. I could have easily made the exchange, but I knew Moreno's reputation thanks to Chambon. He wasn't going to let Carina and me leave peacefully. He was the kind of guy that didn't like witnesses. That would just spell more trouble for him later. I just knew deep down that he was going to kill us both. I also knew now was my chance if we had any hope of escaping.

I lowered my hands like I was going to hand the bags over. Moreno was smiling at how smoothly the transaction was going. He put his hands out like he was ready to take the shipment. Once he was within reach, I threw both bags into the air simultaneously. Moreno's face changed instantly. His smug smile changed to an expression of worry as he watched what remained of his shipment approach the spinning chopper blades.

"No!" he yelled.

Both bags burst instantly. The two gunmen that had their weapons drawn covered their faces as they were covered in the lethal powder. I knew they were goners. I didn't stick around long enough to watch the effects. The other two gunmen covered their faces and hurried to get away from the helicopter. For Levi, it was just too much. The poor Cracker horse turned quickly and darted back in the direction we'd come from.

"Run, Carina!" I yelled.

Carina dashed for the woods, and I followed. She was quick, too! I didn't think I could keep up with my limp and my boots. By the time I finally caught up to her, she had stopped. I saw the light in distance reflecting off the back of her shirt. She was trying to figure out where to go. I grabbed her from behind. She started to scream, and I spun her around so she could see that it was me. I saw her face under the full moon. She was scared to death.

"Colt!" she said. I grabbed her and hugged her tight. Then I kissed her quickly.

"Come on!" I yelled. I grabbed her hand, and she followed. We found some palmettos and ducked down behind them. "Be quiet," I whispered. We were both breathing heavily. The helicopter blades were beginning to slow down. "Their chopper must be damaged."

Carina looked at me, then back in the direction of the helicopter. We could see the lights of the helicopter behind some trees. Some figures crossed the path of the lights. Their shadows stretched eerily into the woods. They were yelling in Spanish.

"I wish I knew what they were saying," I said. "Do you know any Spanish, Carina?"

"A little bit. Enough."

"What are they saying?"

"It's nothing good," she replied.

"What are they saying?" I asked curiously.

"That if you think you're a stallion now, you won't be for long."

"Oh, boy," I said sarcastically.

"You won't be if they get ahold of you."

The lightning from the storm was getting closer. It was reflecting off the trees, and the wind continued to pick up. We could see one of the figures approaching. It was one of the gunmen. I looked at Carina and put my index finger to my mouth as a sign for her to stay quiet. Then we both watched as the man continued to get closer.

"Grab his gun if you get a chance," I whispered.

"What are you going to do?" she said.

"I'm making this up as I go," I replied.

"Oh, no."

I slipped my brass knuckles on my right hand and waited. The man had his weapon pointed forward as he approached cautiously. He didn't know we were here. Right when he was in front of the shrubbery, he stopped and looked around. He decided to head deeper into the woods. That was my cue. I lunged out from the bushes, grabbed him around the neck with both arms, and pulled him back.

The man struggled as he tried to fight me. Carina grabbed the gun, careful not to get in the way of the barrel. Once she had a good grasp on it, she pulled it out of his hands and pointed the gun at us both. Meanwhile, the gunman continued to fight me to break free. With my body weight, I managed to sling him to the side of me. Before he realized what had happened, I took my brass knuckles and started to hit him repeatedly in the face. I finally knocked him out.

"Hand me that strap," I said to Carina. She unclasped the strap from the gun and handed it to me. I turned the man over and tied his hands behind his back. Then I removed his belt and strapped it around his ankles.

"We'll just leave him here for now," I said. "Let me see that."

Carina handed me the gun. I looked at it quickly. It looked to be Russian based on the lettering. I undid the clip and looked inside. There were several rounds left.

"Follow behind me," I said. Carina stayed close as she followed. We slowly walked out from behind the bushes, careful not to make any noise. Another figure was approaching; it was the other gunman. Carina and I took cover behind a large oak tree.

The gunman slowly walked forward with his gun drawn. He stopped just on the other side of the tree and looked around. Carina and I stayed quiet and watched. When he didn't see anything, he decided to move on. I walked out from behind the tree and put the barrel of my gun to his back.

"Don't say a word," I said. He put his hands out, and Carina walked up and grabbed his gun out of his hands. I tapped him in the back twice with my gun barrel to move him forward. He did as directed.

"Remember," Carina told him, "don't say a word." She pointed his gun right at him.

He looked back at me.

"You better listen to her," I said. "She's a hell of a shot."

We laid him down and repeated the same process as before. I tied his hands up with the strap of the gun but used my own belt to tie his ankles since he wasn't wearing one. Then we used his shirt to gag his mouth to keep him quiet. As we sat him down against the oak tree, Carina screamed.

It was Moreno. He had managed to sneak up on us. He had his left arm around Carina's neck and had placed the tip of my revolver to her temple. Carina tried to struggle, but she was no match for the man. I took my borrowed gun and aimed it right at his head.

"Well," he said. "Amazing how the tides have changed."

"Let her go, Moreno!" I said.

"I guess we have ourselves a standoff."

"I swear, Moreno, if you harm her, I'll—"

"You'll what?" he demanded angrily. He cocked the revolver. "If you come anywhere near her, I'm going to blow her brains out. Put the gun down!"

I hesitated. He was right in my sights. I wanted to pull the trigger, but I was worried about hitting Carina.

"Put the damn thing down, now!"

I turned the barrel of the gun down and slowly laid it on the ground in front of me. Then I put my hands out.

"Just don't hurt her," I said.

"To hell with you," he said. "To hell with you and her. Now, who should I kill first? If I kill her, it will torture you. That would be fun to watch." He smiled at that idea.

"Moreno, please don't hurt her. Just let her go. I'll do whatever you want."

"You must really love this girl," he said.

"You can't even begin to imagine."

Carina stopped struggling and watched me.

"I wonder if she feels the same about you." He quickly pulled the gun away and pointed it directly at me.

"No!" Carina screamed.

"Well, what do you know," Moreno said. "She does. Who do I kill first? My, the decisions." A few seconds went by as we stared at one another. "Sorry, Colt! Say goodnight."

Carina screamed and began fighting Moreno. I jumped in to help her. We both began fighting Moreno for the gun. He lifted the gun up into the air to keep it out of our hands. Then we heard a gunshot, but it wasn't from my revolver. It came from behind us. Moreno stopped struggling and fell over backward, dead. I grabbed Carina and held her tight. She was worked up and breathing heavily. I was, too. I was trying my best to calm her down.

We both turned to see where the shot had come from. Out from the brush appeared Sheriff Harding. He didn't say a word. He pointed his rifle down to the ground and walked up to us. Will was right behind him. Carina and I didn't say anything at first. We were still in shock at what had happened.

"You two okay?" Will asked.

"We're a little shaken up," I replied. "But we're okay." Carina didn't say a word. She nodded her head yes, and we continued to hold each other tightly.

Sheriff Harding looked down at Moreno's body. "We've been trying to get this prick since I started with the department decades ago."

"How did you—" I began.

"How did we find you?" Sheriff Harding said. "I knew you would try some of that cowboy hero crap. I just had a feeling you would take things into your own hands if Chambon approached you. So, I had Will keep an eye on you the entire time."

"So, you know about Chambon?"

"I've been keeping an eye on you ever since you left the office," Will said.

"So, you didn't trust me," I replied.

"*You* didn't trust *us*," Will said. "You didn't tell us about the other bags of drugs." I didn't say anything. "It worked out for us, though."

"We figured Chambon was going to approach you," Sheriff Harding interjected. "We decided to put a tail on you and let you play your game. You bought us some much-needed time, though. While you kept Moreno busy and got Carina back, we were able to move in quietly. I hate to say it, but you did a good job."

I tilted my head and smiled a little. I wasn't sure what to say. That was a high praise coming from someone like Sheriff Harding.

~ 22 ~

"I MADE A PROMISE."

As the breeze started to calm down, the storm off in the distance seemed to dissipate. The skies were clear, and the moon above was bright. Patrol trucks and SUVs were parked on both sides of the road, near my truck and trailer. Helicopters circled the woods, looking for other possible suspects, while the Coast Guard went to work capturing Moreno's yacht offshore. The DEA was also present.

As we exited the woods, deputies from the sheriff's office and DEA agents led Moreno's gunmen and pilot out of the woods and put them in the backs of several squad cars parked alongside the road. I managed to find Levi, and Carina and I led him across the street. I tied him to the back of my trailer. Drivers passing through couldn't help but slow down at the sight of all the lights just to catch a glimpse of what was happening.

"Come here, you two," Sheriff Harding said. He opened the tailgate of Will's patrol truck and tapped it with his hand. I helped Carina up, then pulled myself up and sat down on the tailgate. He waved his left hand toward a man with a badge who was dressed in regular clothes. "This gentleman is from the DEA. I need you to start from the beginning. Tell us what the hell happened. I've already filled him in on the basic details."

I gathered myself for a minute. I was trying to figure out where to start. "Basically, it was a drug deal that fell apart. It all became clear when Chambon explained his side of the story. Everything

147

makes a lot of sense now. You see, Mrs. Philippe was the one who called me about her stolen horse, Tempest. I thought the case was odd from the beginning. It's unusual for a known show jumper to be stolen. Think about it. How do you hide it? And she wanted nothing to do with the police. She said she didn't want to get tied up in legal matters. When I began asking her detailed questions that I thought would help in locating Tempest, she started talking about her late husband, almost like she was looking for sympathy."

"In other words," interrupted Sheriff Harding, "it was a distraction."

"Exactly," I said. "Other parts of our meeting didn't make sense either. Tempest, being a show jumper, was on an unusually tight schedule, not to mention the fact that she was an older horse. I also unintendedly mentioned the idea of retirement. Mrs. Philippe never mentioned retirement for Tempest until I said it. Nor did she check on her horse during quarantine. She also said one more thing that was suspicious after I accepted her case. She told me to be careful. That 'they might be dangerous.' How would she know that?"

"Where does Chambon come in?" asked Will. "He was there, too. Right?"

"Chambon was acting as the middleman," I replied. "He was working for Moreno. Moreno wanted to find a new way of shipping drugs into the country so he could regain his market share he lost back in the eighties. He used Chambon to search for horse owners who might be willing to use their animals as mules to make an extra buck."

"So, Mrs. Philippe knew all along," said Sheriff Harding.

"I thought she was an innocent bystander at first," I said. "But Chambon told me that her husband donated most of his wealth to medical research. She received some money and her husband's prized show jumper. According to Chambon, though, she wanted more, and she didn't care for Tempest."

"That old woman mistreated poor Tempest terribly, too," Carina interjected angrily. She was still shaken up over the whole ordeal. "They had the poor thing swallow four bags of carfentanil. They gave her motility drugs to slow her digestion."

"I've seen that before," said the DEA agent. "That's just sick to do to a poor animal. Are you sure it was carfentanil?"

"Yes," Carina replied. "I tested it in my lab."

The DEA agent looked at Sheriff Harding.

"She's a vet," the sheriff said.

"Carfentanil has a high street value," said the agent. "A small shipment could be worth a fortune. How did you first find out about the drugs?"

"After I tracked down Tempest," I continued, "I brought her to Carina's facility. While she was there, she began acting weird. Then she died."

"The poor thing fought as hard as she could, but there was no hope," said Carina. "I had a hunch. I performed an autopsy to find out exactly what happened. That was when I found the drugs. One of the bags had burst."

"It wasn't long after that when you were kidnapped," said Will.

"As it turns out," I inserted, "Chambon decided to steal the drugs and keep them to sell on the streets. He picked the perfect time. You see, he handled all of the logistics for Mrs. Philippe. They both said they didn't see the horse at quarantine, but I found Chambon's signature from when he'd picked up the horse from the facility.

"No one saw him?" asked the agent.

"He tried to stay out of sight," I replied. "He stayed in the cab of the truck. He waited for a busy weekend in Ocala. He was betting that the workers would be so busy at the facility that they would cut corners and miss him. It almost worked. That's when things went south for him. At some point, Mrs. Philippe found out about Tempest being picked up. Chambon pretended not to know anything. She panicked because she didn't want to get on Moreno's bad side. At the same time, Chambon was worried about being caught by Moreno if she said something. To keep her content, he looked me up and forwarded my information to Mrs. Philippe. She in turn put me in charge of the case. He didn't want the police involved, obviously. He was hoping I was some 'dumb redneck,' as he put it. He thought I would eventually give up on the case.

"Looking back at when Chambon kidnapped me, his plan was beginning to fall apart. Chambon was talking on the phone with someone who was worried. He was trying to reassure them that everything was fine and that 'he' didn't suspect anything. 'He' had to be Moreno. As it turns out, Moreno was closing in on him. Unlike Chambon, Moreno was a professional drug dealer. He probably knew what Chambon was up to."

"That's why he was so panicked on the jet," said Will.

"I think so," I said. "He knew Moreno was coming by that point."

"That's also why he wanted to stay off the streets," interjected Sheriff Harding.

"All these drug deals are the same," said the agent. "There are so many backstabbers in this game. Packages change hands all the time. Speaking of packages, the sheriff's office has two, but you had two as well. The ones you threw at the helicopter blades. Was that part of the overall plan?"

I paused for a minute.

"Yes," Sheriff Harding said. "I deputized him so he could transport the drugs and carry out the plan. I directed him, as a deputy, to handle the situation as he saw fit."

"Good work, guys," said the agent. "We'll need to meet again, but I think I'm going to let you guys go so you can head home and get some much-needed rest."

Sheriff Harding and the agent walked off as they discussed a few more details.

"You know," said Will, "I just thought of something."

"What's that?" I asked.

"Did you have a signed contract with Mrs. Philippe?"

"We agreed with a handshake."

Will shook his head and smiled. "You know you're not going to get paid. If anything, she's going to jail."

I stopped and thought about it. "Damn it, you're right! I got so wrapped up in solving the case that I never thought about it!"

"Well, maybe next time," he laughed. Then he headed over to Sheriff Harding and the agent.

I got off the tailgate and looked at Carina. I helped her down, and we began to head back toward my rig.

"You came for me," she said with a smile.

"I made a promise," I said. We stopped and hugged tightly before I looked down at her. "I wasn't going to let anything happen to you." I couldn't help but be drawn into her eyes. We turned our heads slightly and kissed. We both looked at each other again and smiled. "Plus, I needed a place to keep Levi. What would I do if something happened to you?"

I laughed, and she hit me.

"Huh ... Colt, why do I put up with you?"

"Because I like you. I like you a lot."

We hugged each other tightly again as Will approached.

"We were talking," Will said. "Could you two help us with one more thing?"

~ 23 ~

"IT'S YOUR RODEO, GIRL."

Over a week's time, Central Florida had shifted into a dry spell marked by bright sunny days. The kind most tourists dream of when they think of the sunny beaches of Miami or the Keys. The quiet days of Williston resumed as before. Anyone passing through would never have guessed that it had been the epicenter of so much excitement for two days and nights. But one more task remained. It was Carina's turn to settle the score.

"You think this is going to work?" I asked her.

"If she's the way you described," she began, "I guarantee she won't notice the difference."

"She may not be a horse person," I said. "But she should at least be able to tell the difference."

"It's the only horse I could find that looks like Tempest," she replied.

I looked at Carina, halfway unsure. She said, "He's a gelding ... close enough. Besides, if my plan works like it should, we won't have to take him out of the trailer."

"It's your rodeo, girl," I replied. I closed the door to the trailer and secured it. I followed Carina around the trailer and stopped in front of the window where the horse was looking out. I pet his nose. "What's this guy's name?"

"Zephyr," she replied. "He's a young cutter. Just starting out and full of spirit." She pet his nose and gave him a kiss. "Thank you for helping us out." When Carina pulled back, the horse stuck his head out like he wanted more attention. She gave him a treat, and I closed the window once Zephyr retreated back inside.

"His owners don't mind us doing this?" I asked.

"Not at all," she said. "They owe me a favor. And when I told them what happened, they were more than happy to help. They can't stand animals being mistreated, either. It'll be good for him, too. He needs the experience being trailered."

Carina walked over to the rear driver's side window of the truck and gave Duke a couple pats on the head. He was hanging his head out the window, panting and keeping an eye on everything. He was just happy to be there. I could tell he loved the attention. Carina reached into her pocket and gave him a treat. I thought to myself, *It's so good to have her back. Things are just about back to normal.*

"You're due for a pill when we get back," Carina said to Duke. "Colt, don't forget." Then she began making her way around the truck. I couldn't help but watch every curve before she spun around and put her hands on her hips. "Are you coming?"

"Just thinking," I said.

"Well, you can think about that later," she said. "We have to be there at six."

She spun around again, made her way around the front of truck, and climbed into the passenger seat of the cab. I couldn't help but smile. I climbed into the driver's seat, and we began making our way up the gravel road of Carina's facility. Before we turned onto the highway, we noted Will sitting in his police truck in the gravel parking lot of Carina's office. He had a couple of officers with him.

"Looks like Will is ready to go," I said. I looked at him and touched the brim of my Stetson with two fingers, signaling that we were ready. He waved back, meaning he was ready as well. I pulled out onto the highway when it was clear. Will followed behind just far enough to stay out of sight. As we rounded the curve at the water tower, I began taking note of everything in town. It was a nice sunny afternoon. You couldn't ask for a better one.

"Everything looks the same," I said. "Like nothing ever even happened."

"That's the great thing about a small town," Carina replied. "Nothing changes. It always feels like home."

The traffic was beginning to get lighter as everyone headed home for the day. It made for easy driving. Just before we crossed the railroad tracks, we noted Keke waving at us. He was also waving his shirt above his head.

"Why does Keke do that?" I asked.

"I don't know," Carina replied. "He's been doing that for twenty years. He seems content, though."

Outside of town, I picked up speed and began driving at the speed limit of sixty-five miles per hour. We listened to the sounds of the engine humming and Duke panting for a few minutes.

"What did you all do while I was gone?" Carina asked.

"What did we do?" I repeated. "We were worried to death. Between Chambon's silence and his wild goose chases, we had no way of knowing if you were even still alive. We couldn't even find a clue." I shook my head again just thinking of the ordeal. "I'll never let you out of my sight again."

"So, you do like me," she said with a smile.

"Darlin', not one second went by that you were not in my thoughts."

She looked at me and smiled even wider before sitting back in her chair. "Well, just remember one thing."

"What's that?" I asked.

"I told you so."

I closed my eyes for a second and put my head back against the headrest. "You're going to hold that over me forever. Aren't you?"

"Yes, I am!" she replied. "Next time, listen to me."

"For you, darlin', I'm all ears."

She smiled again and began petting Duke with her left hand before gazing out the window.

The heavier traffic in Ocala slowed us some as we entered the city limits, but we managed to make it to the location by the time requested. It was an empty parking lot at an abandoned department store. It was near the airport. I pulled into the lot carefully so that my passengers would not bounce around. Then I circled my rig around and lined up the truck and trailer across multiple parking spots. The front of the truck was facing the entrance of the lot. Carina and I exited the cab to stretch our legs and enjoy the sun.

"Is this the correct place?" Carina asked.

I double-checked the address on my phone.

"This is what she said," I replied. I looked around. "This has got to be it. She's hoping to make this exchange quick and not be seen."

We both leaned against the brush guard and made small talk while we waited.

"Do you think anything is going to happen?" Carina asked.

"With her?" I said. "No, I don't think so. She had no idea what she was getting involved in to begin with."

Just as planned, a Mercedes followed by a truck towing a horse trailer entered the parking lot right at six o'clock. The vehicles circled around and parked alongside my rig. A uniformed driver exited the Mercedes, walked around the vehicle, and opened the rear passenger door for Mrs. Philippe to exit.

"Mr. Callacy," Mrs. Philippe began. She clasped her hands. "I'm so happy to see you are okay." She then hugged me. I could tell it was all a show. I gave Carina a look, and she looked back at me and rolled her eyes. After a few seconds, Mrs. Philippe finally let go.

"I believe there is someone here who wants to see you," I said. I walked over to my horse trailer and opened the window. Zephyr, being nosey, stuck his large head out the window to see what was happening. He looked around at the parking lot.

"My dear Tempest," Mrs. Philippe said. "I would recognize that face anywhere! I was so worried about you! How is my favorite little girl?" She hurried up to the window and tried to hug Zephyr's head. Carina and I both struggled to hide the smirks on our faces. Zephyr shook his head a couple times before retreating back inside the trailer. Mrs. Philippe stood back and thought for a minute. "Well, she always was more of my husband's little girl than mine."

"Mrs. Philippe," I said, "this is Carina. She is the vet I took Tempest to after I located her."

Carina reached out to shake Mrs. Philippe's hand.

"Thank you so much for taking care of my baby," Mrs. Philippe said. "It looks like you took good care of her."

"I gave her a thorough examination," Carina replied. "I know a lot about Tempest. I've been wanting to meet you for a while."

"You're a fan of Tempest?" Mrs. Philippe asked.

"You could say that," Carina said with a smile. She pushed some of her long dark hair behind her right ear with her hand. That was the signal. "I want you to meet someone else who helped us with your baby."

In just a few seconds, the entire parking lot was swarmed with Ocala police. Squad cars of all shapes and sizes blocked every exit. Mrs. Philippe was taken aback as she looked all around her. Her driver and the workers in the truck were clueless as to what was happening. Will pulled up in his truck, exited, and began walking up to us.

"Mrs. Philippe?" he asked.

"Yes?" she replied. The tone of her voice was one of uncertainty.

"You're under arrest for drug trafficking," Will said. "Turn around and put your hands behind your back."

Mrs. Philippe complied as an Ocala police officer began reading her rights to her. Carina smiled. She'd had her day.

We stepped back around to the front of my truck so the officers could do their jobs. Carina and I leaned against the brush guard and enjoyed the sun some more. The crickets and cicadas began singing away off in the distance.

"Good job, you two," Will said as he walked up. "I think you both missed your calling."

"I think I'm happy being a vet," Carina replied.

"I think I'm ready to get back to working small cases again," I said.

Will just smiled. "I think we're done here. You both drive home safely."

"See you later, Will," I said.

Carina and I climbed into the cab of my truck and began making our way out of the parking lot. I looked in the side mirror and saw the officers finishing up their work in the distance before they disappeared out of sight. Once we were outside of town, Carina undid her seat belt, lifted the console between us, and scooted over to the seat next to me. She leaned against me and rested her head on my shoulder as we both stared at the sunset ahead of the truck. In the far distance, we could just make out the metal water tower of Williston. Our home was finally at peace again.

www.ingramcontent.com/pod-product-compliance
Lightning Source LLC
Chambersburg PA
CBHW030933060726
47591CB00005B/1774

9 781965 315163